THE KEY IS LOST

THE KEY IS LOST

BY IDA VOS

Translated by Terese Edelstein

SCHOLASTIC INC.

New York Toronto London Auckland Sydney
Mexico City New Delhi Hong Kong

ISBN 0-439-29137-2

Text copyright © 1996 by Ida Vos.
Translation copyright © 2000 by Terese Edelstein.
Cover copyright © 2000 by HarperCollins Publishers.
Cover illustration copyright © 2000 by Raúl Colón.
All rights reserved. Published by Scholastic Inc.,
555 Broadway, New York, NY 10012, by arrangement with
HarperCollins Children's Books, a division of HarperCollins
Publishers. SCHOLASTIC and associated logos are trademarks
and/or registered trademarks of Scholastic Inc.

12 11 10 9 8 7 6 5 4 3 2 1   1 2 3 4 5 6/0

Printed in the U.S.A.   40

First Scholastic printing, March 2001

For Itamar Vos and Sophie Dajez

HUGUENOTS

HER NAME HAS BEEN EVA ZILVERSTIJN HER whole life long. Until today. In a couple of hours the entire Zilverstijn family must go into hiding from the Germans, who want to kill all the Jews in Holland. Suddenly Eva may no longer be Eva Zilverstijn, but another child with a strange French name.

Twelve years ago her father went to the city hall in Groningen to report that his wife had just given birth to a daughter. "Her name is Eva, sir, and she has dark hair," he said proudly to the official of the registrar.

"Congratulations, Mr. Zilverstijn," answered the man behind the counter. "You've chosen a beautiful name. It sounds good, Eva Zilverstijn."

Three years later Papa returned to the city

hall to report the birth of their second daughter, Lisa Zilverstijn.

Now Eva must get used to being called Marie-Louise Dutour; in addition, she must get used to calling her sister Marie-Jeanne Dutour. Eva can barely remember her sister's new name, and she can hardly pronounce it either. But Ali, who is in the underground, says that these new names are absolutely necessary.

Ali is furious with the Germans because they are making life so miserable for the Jews. That is why she has found a place for the Zilverstijns to hide. "Take the train to Enschede, and I'll meet you by the bicycle shed next to the station," she said. "I'll rent some bicycles, and I'll bring you to a very sweet widow who lives in Losser. You won't be the first Jews I've taken to that village."

The girls must now memorize a story in order to trick everyone into believing that they are not Jewish children. That is why they have taken on those strange French names, because supposedly their ancestors were Huguenots who had to flee from France to Holland. Actually, a little bit of the story is true; however, their ancestors were Jews, not Huguenots, and they fled from Poland instead of from France. In

Poland their name was Silberstein.

Before the war Papa often told them about his Polish family. There was Jankele, his great-great-grandfather, who knew so many wonderful stories that on Christmas the mayor of Proyczeck, where Jankele lived, always summoned him to the town hall to tell them. Later on that same mayor threw Jankele into prison. A townsman spread the rumor that Jankele the Jew had stabbed a Christian baby with a knife and had drunk its blood as though it were wine. When Jankele was free again, he gathered his whole family together to tell them that he no longer wanted to live in Poland. He would try to flee, and that is what he did. He traveled from Poland through Germany, to the northern part of Holland. Along the way he earned some money by pantomiming his stories, for no one could understand him when he spoke in his own language. Jankele crossed over borders until he reached Holland, where he met a nice girl named Golda. When Jankele was ready to marry, he decided to change his last name at the same time, so that no one would know he was a refugee from Poland. Golda and Jankele had eight children, all Zilverstijns. As the years passed, almost no one was aware that the Zilverstijn family had ever been called by another name.

But now the girls must forget their own names, just like their great-great-great-grandparents. The Germans, who invaded Holland in May 1940, are just as mean to the Jews as the Poles were in Jankele's time. They send people to work camps, but Ali says that she doesn't believe they are work camps at all. "I don't know what's going on, but they're not work camps," she said. "Tell me now, what would babies and children do in a work camp?"

Eva thinks that Ali is right. How could a baby peel potatoes or dig up the earth or wash clothes? A baby belongs in its own crib, with a silver rattle in its hand!

Eva and Lisa don't mind going into hiding. The Germans won't let them do anything anyway. They may no longer sit outside on a bench, they are not allowed to ride in a tram or a train, and they may not go to the library, where there is a large sign with JEWS FORBIDDEN written upon it.

Davy and Doortje Baruch are also in hiding,

but that is a big secret that Eva and Lisa are never, ever allowed to discuss with anyone.

They have known Davy and Doortje for only three years. The Zilverstijns had just moved from Rotterdam to Rijswijk, and the girls went out one day to explore their new neighborhood a little bit. They heard some children playing jump rope around the corner. On a bench right by those children sat a boy and a girl. They were Davy and Doortje, who told Eva and Lisa they weren't permitted to play. "We're Jewish, you see. That's why the other children won't play with us. They think the Nazis won't allow it."

When Lisa told Davy and Doortje that she and Eva were Jewish, Davy immediately went to fetch his jump rope. The four of them were soon jumping rope too, and were singing so loudly that the non-Jewish children could no longer hear their own jumping song:

> In, spin, the rope swings in,
> Out, spout, the rope swings out.

All those non-Jewish children could drop dead, as far as they were concerned. It would serve them right!

From then on the four children were together every day until about a week ago, when Davy and Doortje suddenly disappeared. Eva and Lisa must now keep a big secret. Absolutely no one may know that Davy and Doortje are in hiding. No one knows where they are; not even Papa and Mama know. The Baruch family had barely left when the Zilverstijns saw a large moving van marked PULS pull up in front of the Baruchs' home. The men who stepped out of the van proceeded to take all the furniture and books out of the Baruchs' house: Doortje's bed; the chair and pretty dresses of their grandmother, Omi Schillaj; a bookcase . . . everything was loaded into that van and shipped to Germany. All of Davy's and Doortje's possessions belong to the Nazis now.

That's the way it is these days. Jewish children must go to work camps, or they must go into hiding, and there is nothing to be done about it.

The Zilverstijns will have to take the train to Enschede at twenty minutes past four. But what if Ali doesn't arrive at the bicycle shed on time? She didn't tell them who that "very sweet widow" is or even where she lives. What if there are Germans in the train, and what if they ask the girls who they are? Eva will have to say that difficult French name, and what was it again anyway? She can't remember. She doesn't know. She doesn't want another name; she wants to be Eva Zilverstijn. Tomorrow, the day after tomorrow, and forever.

BICYCLING

"ARE YOU ALL RIGHT?" ASKS ALI, LOOKING AT Eva with concern. "You haven't been on a bicycle for such a long time. And you must be hot in that raincoat."

"I'm still shivering a little, from being in the train."

"Was it that bad?" Ali lays her hand on Eva's arm.

Eva nods. "There were Nazis with guns at the station in Enschede, and ordinary policemen too."

"Don't think about it anymore. You're safe now," Ali says, touching Eva's hand. "But you mustn't keep looking back. Your parents and sister are following us. It's safer that way."

Eva's legs are so heavy that she can hardly

pedal. "Wait," says Ali, "I'll push you a bit."

"Papa used to do that too when I was little. Before the Nazis took my new bike away."

"Shh, be careful." Ali brings her hand back to her own handlebar. "Talk about the nice weather or about that pretty river over there. Do you know what it's called?"

"No."

"It's called the Dinkel. But of course you haven't studied geography in a very long time. We're almost there."

"Where?"

"I can't tell you yet. It's better not to. You know what I mean, don't you?"

"Yes. If we're arrested, I can't betray——"

"Shh. You have a lot to learn, my girl."

Eva looks to the side. Ali seems to be angry.

"There it is. Do you see that white house?" asks Ali, pointing in the distance. She glances behind her. "Everything is all right, thank goodness. You poor thing, are you that tired? It's only a little farther. I have something to tell you just before we arrive. You can look forward to a most unusual meeting."

Eva doesn't understand a single thing. What does Ali mean? She is bicycling along a river, without a star on her coat. It is already evening, and she is still outside, and that is absolutely forbidden by the Germans. Jewish children must wear stars, and they must stay inside after eight o'clock, even when the weather is as nice and warm as it is now. What if a German stops her and wants to know her name and destination? What would she say? Her back is soaking wet, her legs can hardly push down the bicycle pedals, and what was that new name again?

Ali seems to be a mind reader. "What's your name?" she asks suddenly.

"Marie-Louise." Eva sighs. Luckily she can still remember it.

"Good," Ali says. "Look, we're here." She steps off her bicycle. "Put your bike against mine. Your parents can lean theirs against that white fence."

"Come in!" calls a woman who is standing in the doorway. She wipes her hands on her flowered apron. "Hurry. Get away from the door."

They enter a large living room. The woman extends her hand. "I'm Geesje," she says, "and this is Henny." She points to a girl in a nurse's uniform. "Henny knows exactly what is going on here. She is Ali's friend. They're in the resistance together. Henny will be leaving as soon as you go upstairs. She has other important things to do."

Geesje slips her hand into Eva's hand. It feels as rough as sandpaper. "Sit down," she says, and points to a big chair. "You can sit by the window, Ali." She points to Papa, Mama, and Lisa. "The three of you must sit as far from the window as possible. First we'll have coffee. Then we'll all go upstairs, to your room."

She looks at Eva. "And you, little maid, you've got to stay away from the window too. You can sit in Grandpa's chair."

Eva is nearly drowning in the huge leather chair. She sees her reflection in the mirror that is hanging above the fireplace mantel. That mirror is tilted so far forward that it looks as though it is going to fall. She notices that she is still wearing her coat. The star has been removed; that feels very strange, because she has had to wear that rotten thing for such a long time. Until now she has never, ever been allowed outside without that big yellow star with the word *JEW* upon it. If she had done so, she could have been arrested and sent to the concentration camp at Westerbork.

Eva slides out of the chair and walks toward Ali.

"Don't!" Someone is pulling on the belt of her raincoat. Eva turns around.

"Yes, it's me," says Henny. "Don't go near the window, remember? Sit back down in Grandpa's chair. And take your coat off. You look as though you're about to leave."

"Where is our room?" asks Papa.

"Upstairs," Geesje replies. "And you won't be alone. Your family won't be alone, that is. There are five others." She winks at Ali. "Do you want to tell them?"

"Then there will be nine of us, Geesje," exclaims Papa. "Isn't it dangerous to be hiding so many people?"

"Not if everyone follows the rules," she answers. "And you'll learn those as a matter of course."

Ali coughs. "Well? Who do you think is upstairs?"

"We don't know, Ali," says Papa. "Tell us."

"Above us, way up in the attic . . . is the Baruch family!"

"Hurray!" Lisa shouts. "Davy and Doortje are upstairs! Now we can play outside, just as we used to."

"It's unbelievable," says Mama. "How wonderful to see them again! Omi Schillaj spends the whole day knitting, I suppose?"

Ali stops smiling all of a sudden. "Alas, Omi Schillaj isn't with them," she says with a sigh. "But you'll hear about it later."

"There are five people," says Eva. "Four in the Baruch family, without Omi Schillaj. Who is the fifth?"

"Coffee first," says Geesje.

Eva leans her head against the back of the chair.

The grown-ups drink coffee, and the children drink hot chocolate. The adult voices sound far away. Eva hears Lisa's voice every now and then. "Not so loud, Marie-Jeanne," someone says. Eva can barely keep her eyes open. In her half-sleeping state it seems as though she is paying a visit somewhere. The hosts are nice, and in half an hour she will have to go home.

"Dear people, let's go upstairs now," she hears Geesje say. "I hope with all my heart that your stay here will be brief. Wait, I've got to take that pipe upstairs. It shouldn't be downstairs at all. Much too dangerous." She walks to a little table that is next to the leather chair and picks up the pipe. It is gleaming white, with a picture of a sailing ship upon it. "Much too dangerous," she grumbles. "How stupid of him."

Eva doesn't understand. How can a pipe be dangerous? It isn't even lit.

"Come, people. Upstairs!" Geesje calls.

Surprise

GEESJE WALKS UP A LONG WOODEN STAIRWAY. Papa and Mama follow, with Eva and Lisa behind them. Ali is last in the procession. They all removed their shoes before climbing the stairs.

"Otherwise the neighbors would hear that there are a lot of people in my house all of a sudden," Geesje explained, "and that would be dangerous nowadays." She and Ali left their shoes in the hall downstairs. Papa and Mama and the children carry theirs with them.

Compared with Geesje's shoes, Ali's shoes look like boats. Ali herself noticed the difference. "It's no wonder that my big shoes attract so much attention," she mused. "I've been called Ali Big Foot for my entire life. Size eleven is pretty remarkable for a woman. By the time I was ten I was already in a size eight. Children used to tease me about it at school, but it doesn't bother me anymore. I have more important things to think about."

They reach the top of the stairs. "Here it is," says Geesje, and she opens a door.

Papa and Mama are the first to enter. Eva hesitates.

"Go on, don't be afraid," says Geesje. "You'll be safe here for the rest of the war. And it's not going to last much longer."

"Let's hope so," says a familiar voice. It is Uncle Samuel Baruch!

"Welcome to our attic palace." Aunt Soesja!

They exchange kisses. Lisa stands hand in hand with Doortje.

"Remember 'In, spin, the rope swings in'?"

"Remember our seder?"

"Remember . . . remember . . . ?"

"Would you show our new arrivals the bathroom, Jan?" asks Geesje.

"All right," Davy answers, and pulls aside a yellow-flowered curtain. "Here is where we wash, and there is the toilet." He points to a reed mat in the corner of the tiny room. "The toilet is behind that mat."

"Is Jan your name now?" Lisa whispers.

"Yes. Jan de Bruin. And yours?"

"Mine is Marie-Jeanne Dutour. And I'm from Rotterdam, not Rijswijk."

"Me too!" exclaims Davy, and he laughs. "I'm from Rotterdam too. We fled after the bombardment. Geesje is supposed to be my real aunt, and Grandpa is supposed to be my real grandfather. We're no longer Jewish."

"Oh . . . how complicated," says Lisa, and she sighs. "Who is Grandpa?"

"I'm Grandpa."

Lisa looks around, but she doesn't see anyone.

"I'm here. Let me just flush the toilet."

They hear the sound of running water coming from behind the mat. Then a man appears. He approaches Ali. "How are you, Ali?" he says. He bows to Papa and Mama. "Welcome . . . welcome. I'm Geesje's father, known to everyone as Grandpa. I've been in hiding here at my daughter's house for four months, sometimes in this room, sometimes in there." He points to a white wall. "And very, very occasionally I go up there!" he says, pointing to the attic roof with the stem of the pipe that he has just lit. "When I can't stand being inside anymore, I go lie down on the roof. Don't ask me why I'm in hiding. Let's just say that I haven't been very nice to the Germans, and now they're looking for me."

"Don't you ever live downstairs?" Lisa inquires.

"No. I stay up here in this attic room. Sometimes I do go downstairs for a little while, but then I have to make sure that I don't leave anything behind in the living room. If the house is raided, the Germans must believe that Geesje lives here by herself. If the situation becomes very dangerous, I hide behind that white wall. There's a cubbyhole there that is normally used to stow away luggage and other things. That will be your hiding place too, if it becomes necessary. And—"

"We're going to jump rope again and spin tops and—" Lisa calls.

"We can't," says Doortje. "We can only play quiet games because we're not allowed to make any noise. And we can't go outside either. We're in hiding, and people who are in hiding can only hide."

"Let's all sit down at the table," says Geesje. "I have to explain the house rules to you. There are approximately five. Rule number one: Always speak softly. Rule two: Always walk in your stocking feet. Rule three: Never go to the toilet when I have company."

"But what if I have to go really badly?" asks Lisa, looking wide-eyed at Geesje.

"Then you'll use the blue bucket that's in the bathroom. It can be emptied after the company has left. Now for rule number four: You are not allowed to talk at all when visitors are here."

Papa drums his fingers against the table. Aunt Soesja looks at him. "Difficult, isn't it?" she says. "You'll get used to it. You'll have to."

Geesje continues to talk, but Eva isn't listening. She can't take her eyes off Papa, for she is afraid that he will say, "Come, it's time to go. I don't like it here. Get the bags. We're going home."

"The bags! Where are our bags?" Eva shouts, completely forgetting rule number one. She sees Papa looking from Mama to Ali and Mama shrugging her shoulders. Ali does the same.

"Left behind . . . in the train!" exclaims Papa, and he pounds on the table. "Totally forgotten because of the strain of the journey."

"And Freekie then?" Lisa hits Papa's hand. "Where is Freekie?"

"In the train too, of course. What a fool I am," he says, slapping his forehead. "Now we have nothing. No nighttime things, no toothbrushes . . . nothing at all."

"We'll ask Henny to rummage up some clothes for all of you," says Geesje.

"Who is Freekie?" asks Grandpa.

"Freekie is a doll," Lisa whispers.

"There are enough dolls in Losser," says Grandpa, and pulls Lisa's pigtail. "Geesje can go out tomorrow and buy you a doll, can't she?"

"No, she can't. Freekie is a puppet. He was made by Mr. Amici Enfanti when we were on vacation in Bilthoven," she sobs. "And now he's in the train. Maybe a horrible German will come along and take him."

"Shh." Uncle Samuel pulls Lisa onto his lap. "When the war is over, we'll all go to Bilthoven together, and we'll ask Mr. Infanti Kanici to make you a new puppet. It will be a nice outing for us. Geesje and Ali and Grandpa may come too." He looks at Lisa. "Thank goodness you're smiling again."

"His name is Amici Enfanti." She laughs through her tears. "And Freekie is very impudent."

"Terribly impudent," says Mama, laughing. "He always says things that Eva and Lisa wouldn't dare say."

"If Freekie were here now, he would ask—he would ask where Omi Schillaj is," Eva whispers. "I know it for sure."

Uncle Samuel looks at Aunt Soesja. She nods.

"Omi Schillaj didn't want to go into hiding because she didn't want to put other people in danger," Uncle Samuel says quietly. "One morning, just before we went into hiding, we found a letter on the table. It was written in Polish. I can't remember it word for word, but it went something like this:

"Dear children,
Thank you for the five wonderful years I spent with you after I fled from Poland. I'm not going into hiding with you. Give my place to someone who is younger than I. I'll go my own way. Don't worry about me. Everything will be all right."

Uncle Samuel is silent.

"Come, let me tell you about rule number five," says Geesje.

BEING IN HIDING IS FUN!

BEING IN HIDING IS MUCH NICER THAN BEING AT home.

Four months ago, when Eva and Lisa were still in their own house in Rijswijk, the Germans wouldn't let them do anything. They couldn't take a train, they couldn't go to school with non-Jewish children, and they couldn't shop except between three and five o'clock. Actually, Jewish children weren't allowed to do a single thing. Each day they also heard the grown-ups whisper about people who were sent to Westerbork and Poland, people who were simply taken out of their homes by big, strong men. That is still happening, of course, but at least the girls can pretend they don't know about it now. Ali doesn't talk about people who have been arrested. When she visits them in the attic, she talks only about funny things, and she always comes loaded with toys, books, colored pencils, and much more. She brings material for the adults too: tobacco, magazines, and jigsaws and wood for making various sorts of dolls and animals.

"Do they sell all that under the ground?" Doortje asked Ali.

Ali patted her on the cheek and told her that she lived in an ordinary house. "It's not under the ground," she explained. "That's just a term we use these days. My belonging to the under-ground only means that I secretly do things that the Germans have forbidden."

The nicest part about being in hiding is that they are with Davy and Doortje day and night. During the day the four children play quietly in their own little spot in the bathroom, leaving only when someone must use the toilet. In the evening the children and the grown-ups quietly sing songs of long ago. When they sing together, it seems as though they were not up in the attic room but were back home in Rijswijk, visiting one another until late at night.

Grandpa knows many sad songs. There is the

one about Dirkie's little dog, who runs away and is struck down by a car. The saddest song of all is called "On the Wall of the Old Cemetery." It is about a boy who is crying because his mother has passed away. When Grandpa sings it in his deep voice, everyone is dead still. When he comes to the part where the little boy asks God, "When is my mother coming back?" they all have tears in their eyes, even the grown-ups.

Sometimes the day seems very long indeed, for the children must always remain upstairs. Mama and Aunt Soesja are lucky because they are allowed to go downstairs and help Geesje with the cooking nearly every day. When the women are back upstairs, the children like to guess what they will be eating that afternoon. They say the silliest things: herring with whipped cream or pudding with salmon. Then they laugh so hard that the adults call out, "Shh!," all at the same time.

Davy is very clever at making up games. He has fashioned a hand puppet out of a pink washcloth. He embroidered eyes and a mouth, and when he puts his hand inside the little doll, it becomes alive. He has named it Albert.

"He's just like our Freekie," said Eva when

she heard Albert talk for the first time. "Freekie used to say crazy things too."

Lisa asked her sister not to say anything more about Freekie. She becomes terribly sad whenever she is reminded of her doll, which surely belongs to a German child now. "Freekie is probably speaking in German," she said gloomily.

Davy and Doortje know Freekie too. Eva and Lisa are glad of that, for they don't have to explain anything about the past. Together in the bathroom they whisper about the people they know: about Uncle Dries, who was killed in the concentration camp at Mauthausen, and about Omi Schillaj, who didn't want to go into hiding. Then, all of a sudden, Albert pops up with something funny to say.

"Ha, you crazy people, do you know what happens when Hitler makes a speech?" says the little puppet in a squeaky voice.

"No!" the three girls call out.

"Then listen. When Hitler makes a speech, he gets so wound up and he shouts so loudly that he ends up peeing all over himself!"

"He pees all over himself!" Lisa says, and howls with laughter. The others laugh too.

"Shh!" hiss the grown-ups. "You're making far too much noise."

"Albert is the one making noise, not us," Doortje screams.

Grandpa enters the bathroom and sits on the floor next to them. "I advise you not to make such a racket," he whispers. "Geesje is having a hard enough time as it is, with so many people above her head. She can't do anything about it either. She is often afraid that we'll be caught."

"We'll be as quiet as a real washcloth," Albert says.

Grandpa looks so serious that they no longer dare laugh. "Go back into the room," Grandpa says. "I need to be alone in here for a little while."

"May we go into the cubbyhole?" Lisa asks. "We don't feel like being with our parents."

"All right," says Grandpa, "and be quiet, remember?"

One by one the children disappear behind the white brick wall, to the hiding place where they must go in case of danger. They are using it as a play area now. They brought along some candles and two boxes of matches, even though that is not allowed. Each child knows that it's dangerous to play with fire in a closed space.

"I have an idea," Davy whispers. "A long time ago we went on vacation to France, and there in a cave we saw pictures that were made millions of years ago. We're going to make cave pictures too."

"We don't have any paint," Doortje whispers.

"That doesn't matter. We don't need paint," he says, and strikes a match. The small flame lights up the hiding place.

"More matches," he whispers.

"How many?" Eva asks softly.

"Five."

Eva puts five matches in Davy's hand. He takes one, coats it in melted candle wax, and sticks it on the wall.

"What are you making?" Lisa whispers.

"A house," he replies. "You can make something too."

They make another house, a square, and a table. Soon the wall of the hiding place is covered with matches. By the time they are used up, the candles are burned out too. It is pitch black now.

"Shall we go back to the room or to the bathroom?" asks Doortje.

"Let's wait awhile," says Davy, and he pulls his sister back to the floor. "Let's listen to what they're saying. We can pretend that we're clever spies and that we're about to uncover a gang of thieves. I'm Dick Bos, the chief spy."

No one moves. People who catch thieves must be able to sit without moving a muscle.

"Listen to my advice." Grandpa's voice. "Geesje can't bear it any longer. I know my daughter. We'll have to find another solution. Henny will be coming tonight. We'll ask her if she has another place for one family."

"We'll have to leave," Lisa whispers. "And I don't want to. We've got to stay together and make more cave paintings."

"Shh," says Davy, and he puts his hand over her mouth. "Wait. Listen, your mother is saying something."

"Which family will have to go?" they hear.

"It doesn't matter." Grandpa's voice. "We'll draw lots when the time comes. That's what Geesje and I have decided, more or less."

"We're not going away," says Doortje, and she draws close to Lisa.

"We're not going either. We're going to stay together always. Until the war is over," says Lisa, and she takes Davy's hand.

"Shall we make a promise to each other?" Davy whispers. "We'll pile our hands together and make a pledge. I'll think up the words, and when I've finished saying them, you'll answer, 'We promise.'"

They grope in the dark and pile their hands up high. Then Davy speaks: "We, Doortje and Davy Baruch, and Eva and Lisa Zilverstijn, do solemnly swear to stick together and be best of friends forever and ever."

"We promise," they declare together, and it sounds very stately.

"Time to eat, children!" Grandpa's voice.

"Don't tell them that we know," Davy commands.

"We promise," whispers Eva.

"We promise too," Doortje says, and giggles.

LOTS

"I'm sorry," says Uncle Samuel. "We've drawn lots fairly. I think it's terrible that you have to leave. We'll have to separate when Ali comes, so let's say our good-byes now."

He embraces Mama and gives Papa a kiss. "Good-bye for now. See you after the war. Good-bye, dear Lisa. Good-bye, my brave Eva."

"See you after the war," says Davy.

"Where is Doortje?" asks Aunt Soesja. She looks under the table, but Doortje isn't there.

"Leave her alone," Uncle Samuel whispers. "Doortje is in the hiding place. She can't stand to say good-bye."

The Zilverstijns sit at the table with their coats on. Next to Mama is the reed shopping basket that Ali gave to them a while ago.

"This is for you in case you have to flee to another address, but I hope you never reach that point," she said, and placed two baskets in the middle of the table. "There, one for each family."

"Why isn't Ali here yet?" Mama speaks in a strange, high-pitched voice. "She should have been here by now."

They sit in silence, hardly daring to look at one another.

"She's been caught," Lisa whispers.

"We can still switch places," says Aunt Soesja. "Shall *we* leave?"

"Don't even think of it," says Papa. "Fair is fair. We drew lots." He stands up and begins to walk back and forth. "In any case you'll have more room with four fewer people."

"For God's sake, sit down," snaps Mama. "All that pacing is making me a nervous wreck."

They hear footsteps on the stairs. Geesje and Ali enter the room.

"I'm going to sit down for a minute, and then we'll go," says Ali. "Luckily I know people who know some other people who have found an address for you. The entire Zilverstijn family will be in one place. You don't see that very often these days. Many are afraid . . . "

Geesje has remained standing. Her cheeks are flushed, and her eyes are red.

Father puts his arm around her. "We think it's awful, but we understand," he says softly. "If your husband were still alive, you might have been able to withstand the pressures. So many people in your house . . . so dangerous."

"It hasn't even been a year since he—"

"Shh, we know. We understand, and we think you're very brave."

"Shall we go?" Ali stands up. "Come, people."

"Good-bye, Doortje!" Lisa shouts. "See you when the war is over!"

"Walk quickly," says Ali. "We'll take various shortcuts, but it will still be at least an hour and a half before we reach Enschede." She is in front with the children. Their parents follow.

"Why can't we go by bicycle?" Lisa pants. "That's how we got to Geesje's house."

"Too dangerous," says Ali quietly, "and it would attract too much attention. Children your age can normally bicycle very well. But you've been inside for such a long time that I'm afraid you wouldn't be able to manage it."

"It's a shame," Eva says with a sigh.

"I think so too." Ali presses Eva against her. "'A shame' is an understatement. I think it's horrible."

"My feet," groans Lisa. "My shoes are too little for me."

"Do you want to wear mine?" says Ali, and she laughs. "You could certainly fit into mine. You and your sister *together* could fit into my size-eleven shoes." She looks at the girls. "You can still smile, thank goodness."

They walk for a long time. No one has much to say.

"When will we finally be in Enschede?" Lisa whines.

"Now," Ali replies. "I wanted to surprise you. That's why I haven't told you how far we've gone."

"I thought we were in Oldenzaal," says Eva. "Look, that street sign is marked Oldenzaalstraat."

"That butcher shop belongs to Jacques and Trude Butcher." Ali points. "Not only is he named Butcher, but it's his trade too. No one believes it."

She points to a shopwindow that contains tables, chairs, and beds. "And over there is a furniture store owned by Mr. De Beer."

"But there are other names on the store-fronts," Eva remarks.

Ali is silent.

"I know what happened," exclaims Eva. "They were all sent to Westerbork."

Ali looks behind her. "All is well, thank goodness. Do you see that house with the lace curtains? That's where we have to go."

They walk a bit farther and stop in front of the house that Ali pointed out to them. Eva looks back.

Ali pulls on the copper bell. "Look in front of you, Marie-Louise. Your parents are coming." She takes Eva by the shoulder and turns her face toward the door.

"G. M. Drabbelman lives here," says Lisa. "It says so on the door."

They have no time to read whatever else is engraved on the little copper plate, for the door has opened.

"Come in," says a man. "Drabbelman is the name. My wife, Eleonora, will be here in a moment. Step inside, and we'll continue with our introductions."

"I'm Marie-Louise Dutour," says Eva after she has entered. She extends her hand.

The man takes her hand without looking at her. "Who are you?" he asks, staring at Ali.

"I'm Ali."

"Last name?"

"It's not important. Ali is enough."

"And I'm Marie-Jeanne Dutour," says Lisa, and she extends her hand as well.

Mr. Drabbelman studies her in silence.

"Really," says Lisa. "I'm not fibbing. My name really is Marie-Jeanne."

The man doesn't say a word. He walks to the window, pulls the curtain aside, and peeks out. "Two more are coming, I see. That must be Father and Mother Dutour."

"Mission accomplished, thank God," says Ali, and wipes her forehead. "Many, many thanks to you and your wife for taking in these people—"

"You don't have to thank me," Mr. Drabbelman says, interrupting. "I'm not taking them in because I like Jews. I'm doing it because I want to undermine the German regulations as much as I can. I'll do whatever it takes to go against those Nazis."

Eva looks at her father. Here it comes. Papa will be furious now and will tell Ali that he won't stay in the home of a man who says such mean things.

Papa is silent. His face is as white as the lace curtains.

"I'll take them to their room as soon as you've left," Mr. Drabbelman says to Ali.

"I'm going now." Ali gives each of them a kiss.

"Be good," she whispers in Papa's ear. "And be strong."

DRIBBEL...DRABBEL...

WHEN ALI DELIVERED THE ZILVERSTIJNS TO THEIR new address, she said that Papa and Mama must pretend to be members of the Drabbelman family. "For safety's sake," she said. Therefore they must call the Drabbelmans Cousin Gerard and Cousin Eleonora.

Eva and Lisa must call them Uncle Gerard and Aunt Eleonora. Once again they must pretend that they have fled from Rotterdam, and once again they must trick themselves into thinking that their names are no longer Eva and Lisa. If the war lasts much longer, they may well believe that their names *are* Marie-Louise and Marie-Jeanne; Eva and Lisa Zilverstijn would then disappear from the face of the earth.

The girls think it's terrible that they have an

Uncle Gerard and Aunt Eleonora now. They would much rather have their own aunts and uncles back. Uncle Dries and Aunt Sophie, for example, and Uncle Bruno, who fled from Germany and died at Grandpa and Grandma's house in Stadskanaal. They don't know whether any other aunts and uncles have died, for they haven't received news about other people for a long time.

Aunt Eleonora is nice, and she has beautiful curls. Uncle Gerard isn't nice at all. He tells jokes about Sam and Saar, just as Emma's fiancé used to do. Before the war Emma was their cleaning woman when they lived in Rotterdam. Eva was very young at the time, but she knew that those jokes had something to do with Jews. She didn't understand them then, and she doesn't understand them now either.

When Uncle Gerard has told a joke, he laughs so hard that the gold watch that dangles on a chain over his stomach shakes right along with him. When he has stopped laughing, he slaps Father across the shoulder. "That was a good one, wasn't it?" he says. "But where is your famous sense of humor? You're not laughing at all."

It seems as though Papa doesn't understand those jokes, for he never laughs at them and he never has anything to say in return. The last time Uncle Gerard told a joke, Papa remained silent as usual.

"What dull girls you are, just sitting here like two little old women," Uncle Gerard exclaimed then. "Go outside and play. Go on!" He slapped Eva on her bottom. "Get moving!"

The gold watch laughed along with him, but Eva and Lisa could hardly keep the tears from coming. Children in hiding aren't allowed to go outside, and it was very cruel of Uncle Gerard to suggest that they do so. The next day Lisa told her mother that she had had such a strong urge to slap Uncle Gerard that she had to bury her fists under her skirt.

Uncle Gerard is not at home very much, thank goodness. He has a job in a factory. Sometimes he works during the day, and at other times he works at night.

It is boring to be alone with their parents. Mama does a lot of embroidery, and all Papa does is read and sleep. He is sleeping right now. His head is resting on a book that is lying open on the table. Now and then he snores a little;

otherwise it is so quiet that the girls can hear the sound of the rain outside.

"Shall we play a game?" Lisa whispers.

"I don't know any." Eva bites down on her pencil. "What do you want to play?"

"Let's make a bet. Which raindrop will drip down first, this one or that one?" Lisa points to two big drops on the windowpane.

"That one."

"Fine, then I'll bet on the other one. Whoever wins . . .whoever wins . . ." Lisa looks as though she is having pleasant thoughts indeed. "Whoever wins may run up and down the street three times, in the rain," she announces. "And after that the winner may shout very loudly for five minutes. So loudly that she'll become hoarse."

"Can't. We're not allowed to shout." Eva keeps drawing. "Don't be so silly, Lisa."

"I'm not silly, I'm bored. I want to be with Davy and Doortje. I want to go outside."

"Who wants to go outside?" Papa says sleepily.

"*I* do," says Lisa.

"You know that you can't. Do you want to be caught, Lisa?"

"Yes, I do. Then I'd be sent to Westerbork and I would see a whole lot of children from my class, and Grandpa and Grandma too."

"You don't mean that, do you, Lisa?" asks Mama, and she sets her needlework on the table. "Shall we all play a game together?"

"What kind?"

"A rhyming game?"

"No. That's the only kind of game we play."

"Then what?" Mother grasps her embroidery.

"I don't know. It's almost December the fifth."

"What are you trying to say?"

"December the fifth is the birthday of St. Nicholas," says Lisa. "I want to get a present, and I want to give presents to all of you too."

Mama doesn't answer. Papa has gone back to sleep.

"Shall we do something mean?" Eva whispers.

"I don't care," says Lisa, and she lays her head down on the table.

"Shall we make up some rhymes? Some really mean rhymes?"

Lisa looks at her sister. "How?"

"You know that we always write poems for

the holiday of St. Nicholas," Eva replies. "We'll make up some poems, and we'll say some mean things in them. I'll start. Papa and Mama aren't allowed to listen."

"I don't hear anything," says their mother. She picks up her embroidery again. "And Papa can't hear anything because he's sleeping. For just this once you may say some mean things."

"Then here we go," says Eva. "I'm going to make up a mean poem about Uncle Gerard. I haven't decided what to give him. . . . Oh, I have an idea! I'll give him some glue so that he can glue his mouth shut.

"Dear Mr. Drabbelman,
St. Nick has pondered long and deep
To find the right gift for a creep,
So he's decided to give to you
This handy little jar of glue.
Now what on earth will you do with this stuff?
You'll glue your mouth shut. That's enough!"

The girls burst out laughing.

"Not so loud. Don't laugh so loud." Papa raises his head a little, then goes back to sleep.

"Now my turn," says Lisa, still laughing. "I'm

going to be mean too. I'll give Uncle Gerard . . .
I'll give him . . . I don't know what I'll give him.
Maybe just a poem.

> "St. Nicholas was eating soup
> While sitting in a pile of poop.
> Then he cried out, 'Oh, oh, oh,
> Who, oh, who, does stink here so?'
> When there is such an awful reek,
> A lovely gift I cannot seek
> For Dribbel . . . Drabbel. . . Drabbelman,
> The meanest person in the land!"

"What's that?" says Papa, and he pounds his
fist on the table. Then he walks toward Mama. "I
don't understand why you think it's all right for
them to talk that way. You thought I was
sleeping, but I heard Eva's poem too. Shame on
you. Writing such nasty poetry about a man who
is risking his own life by taking us into his house.
Shame on you!"

"I want to leave," Lisa cries. "I want to go
home. I'm afraid of that Dribbel . . . Drabbel . . .
Sorry." She buries her face in her hands. "I can't
help it, the words just slipped out."

Something happens that used to happen a

long time ago, when they were still living at home in Rijswijk. All four of them laugh so hard that they can't stop. Papa stuffs his handkerchief in his mouth, and Mama presses her embroidery to her face.

"Ouch, the needle. My lips . . ." she shrieks.

A door opens downstairs.

"Quiet!" Uncle Gerard calls. "Mouths shut, otherwise . . ."

"Otherwise I'll glue your lips together." Lisa hiccups.

Playing Tag

THE DOORBELL RINGS AT NINE-THIRTY EVERY morning. They can hear Aunt Eleonora run to the hall. "Hurry, the coast is clear," she says to her visitor then.

Eva and Lisa know they must be dead still when Mr. Tag comes to visit. That is what they've named the man who comes over each day. They have never seen him, of course, but they know for sure that he and Aunt Eleonora play tag. The girls can hear them running through the living room, and Aunt Eleonora is never fast enough. "I've got you!" they hear Mr. Tag shout, and then it is quiet for a while. They must be drinking coffee and having a cookie or a pastry with it perhaps.

Eva and Lisa would like very much to go

downstairs and drink coffee with Mr. Tag and Aunt Eleonora, but they know that's impossible. Mr. Tag mustn't know that there are people hiding away upstairs. What a shame.

Nine-thirty. The doorbell.

Aunt Eleonora's heels tap against the tile floor in the corridor. The door opens.

"Here I am again," says Mr. Tag. "Is everything all right, my little curly top?"

The girls can't hear what Aunt Eleonora says. The living room door creaks, then slams shut. They are making a great deal of noise today.

"Here!" Mr. Tag calls. "Stay where you are, Eleonora!"

"Catch me!" she shouts. Then it is quiet.

"Shall I tell you a story?" Papa whispers. "There was once a farmer who was so rich—"

"Not now," Eva whispers. "Later, when Mr. Tag has left. I want to hear them. Why are you smiling, Mama?"

Mama doesn't answer. She bends over her embroidery.

"That farmer was so rich that he gave his wife a gold ornament every week," Papa continues. "Imagine what kind of jewelry she received, and write it down. Wait, I'll get some pencils and paper."

He slides his chair back and begins to tiptoe to the cupboard.

"Watch out, don't trip over your shoes!" Eva warns, but it is too late. She wasn't able to speak loudly enough. Papa is lying flat on his stomach.

"I'm all right," he whispers. "There's nothing broken."

Eva looks at Lisa and sees that she is trying not to laugh. Eva tries too, but it's no use. They begin to shriek with laughter.

"Shh. Are you laughing or crying?" asks their mother, and she begins to laugh a bit as well.

"I don't know. I'm laughing, I think." Lisa wipes the tears from her face. "Don't just lie on the floor, Papa. Get up."

"Be as quiet as you can be," he says. He turns over on his side and puts his ear to the floor. "I can hear them talking, Eleonora and that man. I hear my name. I think it's a good thing that I fell down."

What does Papa mean? They don't dare move. What does he hear? He looks so serious.

"Later," he whispers. "I'll tell you after he's left."

Mama's needlework is lying on the table, with the needle protruding from an embroidered sunflower. Papa's book is lying next to it, his glasses acting as a bookmark on page 131.

They hardly breathe. They know for sure that something terrible is happening downstairs, for they can see it on Papa's face.

"Papa," Eva whispers.

"Shh, mouth shut." He raises his head a little. "I'll tell you later."

They hear Mr. Tag's deep voice and Aunt Eleonora's high-pitched one. Now and then both voices are raised together, but the girls can't understand what is being said.

"He's leaving." Papa stands up carefully. "Listen. They're in the hall."

"Get out," they hear Aunt Eleonora say. "And don't you ever come back. Dirty, rotten traitor. How dare you?"

"You'll hear more about this, my little lady. Adieu!" Mr. Tag's voice. The door slams shut.

"What is it? Why are you so white?" Mama stands in front of Papa and begins to shake him by the shoulders. "Tell us. Don't keep us in such suspense."

"He knows—he knows that we're here. I'll

try to repeat exactly what I heard. He said—"
Papa can hardly talk. "He said, 'We'll go to the
SD together. We'll tell those German police that
your husband has taken in Jews against your will
and that you don't share his views. Then they'll
all be arrested, he and his four Jews. He doesn't
really like them anyway. You yourself said that the
only reason he took them in was to undermine
the German regulations. Then we can be
together forever, my darling. Forever . . . day and
night, for the rest of our lives.'"

"The children. This is not a story for
children," says Mama, and she puts her hand over
Papa's mouth.

He pulls her hand away. "Yes, they must hear
this. We can't keep everything hidden from
them. Well, you heard the rest when they were
standing in the hall—"

"We'll have to get away from here as soon as
possible." Mama puts on her shoes. "Immediately.
Shoes on, everybody, and leave everything as it is.
That wonderful Mr. Tag will naturally go to the
Sicherheitsdienst to turn us all in, including his
darling Eleonora. Where are we to go?"

"We'll go . . . we'll go . . ." Papa takes Mama's
head between his hands. "You know that Ali gave

me two addresses for use in case of emergency. Those addresses are safely hidden away up here." He taps his forehead. "They're in here, and no one is going to get them out."

"Not even if we're caught?" asks Eva.

"Not even if we're caught, Eva. But we won't be caught."

"Never mind," Eva says. "I want to get away from here."

"We'll tell Eleonora that we want to leave," Papa says. "We'll say that we have another address and that we'll never betray her. We'll tell her as soon as she brings us our meal."

"We won't betray her even if we're tortured," says Lisa bravely.

"I'll make sure that nothing happens to us," says Papa. "We won't be caught, and we won't be tortured. I promise."

"I don't believe you," says Eva. "Fathers can't promise anything."

LISA RUNS

THEY WALK DOWN THE STREET IN BROAD daylight, two by two, with Father and Eva leading the way. Papa is carrying a large shopping bag, just as he did when they first went into hiding. Mama is carrying a bottle of milk that Aunt Eleonora gave to her right before they left. They haven't taken much with them, only some underwear, a box of toothpaste, toothbrushes, and a comb. Just as they did when they first went into hiding, they have covered their things with a large head of endive, so that everyone will think that they are an ordinary father and mother who have just been to the grocery store with their children.

"I miss Freekie all of a sudden," Eva says. "He sat on top of the endive when we took the train to Enschede."

Papa doesn't answer.

They continue walking. Left . . . right.

"Did you say something, Papa? Speak louder." Eva pants. He is walking so fast that she can barely keep up with him. "My feet don't want to walk, Papa. They're hurting me."

"When the war is over, you'll get the biggest and most beautiful shoes in the world," he says. "Yours are much too small, and Lisa's are too. Now don't talk anymore. I'm going over the addresses that Ali gave me, and I don't want to be disturbed."

Eva is silent. Now and then she glances back to see if Mama and Lisa are following.

"When we used to take walks, it was always so cozy because the four of us walked alongside together," she says quietly. "Other people could hardly get past us. The whole sidewalk was full of Zilverstijns. And—"

"But now we have to pretend we don't belong together. It's safer that way," Father whispers in her ear.

"If you and I were caught, there would still be two left," she says.

"Shh." Papa says something else, but Eva can't understand him. His lips move as though he were praying, just as Ali does before eating.

She remains silent. Imagine if her father were to forget the addresses because she was talking so much. They would have to spend the rest of eternity on the street, without a house and without a bed.

Eva laughs as she watches a heavy boy pulling along a small white poodle. The harder he pulls on the red leather leash, the more obstinate the dog becomes.

"Never mind!" the boy says, and he laughs. He picks up the dog and puts it in a large reed basket. The little head with the black eyes peeks out above the rim.

"Keep walking."

"In a minute, Papa."

"Keep walking, I tell you."

Eva must continue on whether she wants to or not. Her feet are hurting more than ever.

"Lisa!" A shout, then the sound of breaking glass.

"Lisa, come here!" Mama's voice.

Eva and her father look back. Mama is standing in the middle of a puddle of milk. The broken bottle is lying on the ground next to her.

"Lisa!" Mother screams.

They walk back to Mama. Father grasps her by the shoulders.

"Where is Lisa?" he asks.

"Gone," she sobs. "We'll have to look for her. All of a sudden she ran back to the street from where we'd just come. I couldn't hold her back and—" She pounds her fists against Papa's chest. "Don't just stand there. Do you want her to be caught? Do something!"

"Stay with your mother, Eva," he says. "Go look in the shop windows, and act as though it's normal for you to be outside. Wait for me by the bookstore across the street."

Papa disappears.

Eva takes her mother by the arm. "Come on," she says quietly. "We'll pretend to go shopping. We're just standing here in this puddle of milk, and everyone is looking at us."

Mama lets herself be pulled along a bit, but then she stops. She looks at Eva without really seeing her. "It's a shame about the milk," she whispers. "A shame about that expensive milk. And that broken bottle . . ."

"It doesn't matter. We'll get more milk," says Eva. She tries to encourage her mother to move along, but it's no use. Mama is standing there in an unfamiliar street in broad daylight and is talking to herself as though she were all alone in the world.

"If you don't go with me, we'll be caught," Eva whispers in her ear. "Papa will be coming with Lisa soon, and *we* won't be here because we'll have been arrested. Please come with me."

She has persuaded her mother at last. Mama shuffles across the street. They are standing in front of the bookstore window, where all kinds of books are on display. Eva gazes at a poster that is hanging in the window. On it is a huge photograph of Hitler. Printed underneath in big fat letters are the words *Adolf Hitler*, Mein Kampf. *German edition (741st printing) available here, as well as the Dutch translation by S. Barents.*

Eva stares at Hitler's face. She shuts her eyes, opens them again, and looks at her mother. Luckily Mama hasn't seen the poster.

"Look, Mama. There's *The Cabinboys of Bontekoe*. I used to have that book, remember?" Eva tries to get her to talk, but she can't. Mama is not looking at the books; she is looking at something else in the store.

"There!" she screams, and points. "There he is!"

Eva tries to see what Mama is pointing to.

"There! That soldier! That's why Lisa ran away. He began to approach us, and when he was very close, Lisa became so frightened that she ran away. All he wanted was directions to the Graaf van Speestraat."

"Stop! Don't shout. Keep looking at the books!" Eva exclaims, and pinches her mother's hand as hard as she can. Mama's outburst has startled her so much that she can scarcely breathe. Perhaps they will never see Papa and Lisa again. What would they do then? Where would they go?

"Papa, please come back, please come back with Lisa," she would like to shout, but she holds her tongue. She keeps staring into the window. She sees colors and letters but can no longer read the book titles; the letters are beginning to swim all around, and the colors are too.

Eva rubs her eyes. "Be brave," she tells herself. In the windowpane she sees the reflection of a horse and wagon coming by and something else as well. Quickly she turns around. Papa, Lisa! She can barely keep from shouting aloud. She bites down on her lip and waves.

"Mama, there they are!"

"Who?"

"Papa and Lisa."

"Oh."

"Say something, Mama. Answer me."

"I've got her." Papa and Lisa are now standing in front of the bookstore too.

"Mama, I'm back," Lisa whispers.

"A German soldier frightened her," he says softly. "She thought that he was going to arrest her."

Mama seems to have awakened all of a sudden. "Lisa, you're back," she says in a very strange voice. "Never, never run away again, Lisa . . . Lisa."

"She was far away," says Papa. "All the way in the Graaf van Speestraat. Come on, let's keep going. Eva, you walk with your mother. I'll keep an eye on Lisa. We're almost at Ali's house in the Javastraat."

"Now I know where we're going," says Eva. "But if we're arrested, I won't tell."

Papa looks at Mama. "Don't talk like that," he whispers. "You're upsetting your mother."

IT REALLY IS IMPOSSIBLE

THE DOOR TO ALI'S HOUSE OPENS A TINY CRACK. "What do we have here? Quick, come in." Ali opens the door all the way.

"Lisa was gone and Mama was so upset and I saw Hitler," Eva blurts out. "And then—"

"Wait, not everything all at once." Ali pushes Mama inside. Papa, Eva, and Lisa follow.

"Take off your coats. I'll bring them upstairs. Go sit down for a minute." She drapes the coats over her arm. "I'll be right back."

"We can't stay here," Eva whispers. "She said, 'Go sit down for a minute.'"

"Keep your mouth shut. We'll see," snaps her father.

"Look at that . . . over there . . . that painting . . . it's our clown." Lisa can hardly get the words out.

"Yes, it's the clown that Mr. Amici Enfanti painted for you," says Papa. "We gave it to Ali the night before we went into hiding."

"What a sweet little clown," says Lisa, and she sighs. "And Mr. Amici Enfanti is a wonderful painter, isn't he?"

"I have a problem," says Ali when she is downstairs again. "I can understand that this is an emergency; otherwise you wouldn't have been out on the street during the daytime."

"This *is* an emergency," says Father. "You certainly could call it that. Eleonora's lover wants to go to the Sicherheitsdienst and turn us in. Maybe he has already been there."

Ali looks from one to the other. "Dear people, I'd like very much to keep you here, but it really is impossible. Tomorrow I have to—I'm going . . . four children . . . No, I'm not allowed to say. It would be too dangerous."

"We're homeless, Ali," says Mama, and she grasps her by the hand. "We don't know where to go. I think it might be better if we turned ourselves in to the SD. Then we would no longer have to worry about being caught."

"Stop talking like that," Ali admonishes her. "Thomas, I gave you one other address, didn't I?"

"Yes, it's here in my head," Papa replies.

"Walk to that address. Do you remember where it is? Go to the grocery store, and turn right. There are two display windows, one in my street and one around the corner. After you turn that corner, turn left and then . . ."

Papa walks up to Ali and whispers something in her ear. She nods.

"Good," she says. "That's it. Henny knows the address too. Do you believe me when I tell you how unhappy I am that I don't have room for you here?"

They all nod.

What if those other people aren't at home? Where do we go then? Eva thinks. She is so afraid of what Ali might answer that she can't bring herself to ask. "I don't know where you're to go either," Ali will say, and they will be out on the street again.

"Wait," says Ali. "I'll phone them. Don't be alarmed. I have to inform them in a special way that I'm seeking shelter for four Jews."

She dials some numbers. "Hello, this is Ila," she says. "I have four pair of shoes remaining. Do you want them? . . . Yes, one pair of men's shoes, one pair of women's shoes, and two pairs of children's shoes."

She is silent for a while. She stares at the clown. Then she begins to speak again.

"Good . . . yes . . . hmm . . . I'll tell them. I'll make sure you get them. You're certain that your husband wants them?" Silence. "Good. As long as you're certain, I'll send them."

"It's all been arranged," says Ali after she hangs up the telephone. "You'll go when it's dark. It will be better if I don't go with you. You may stay here until this evening."

She walks over to the clown and removes the picture from the wall. "Here," she says. "Take it to your new address. It can be your mascot." She wraps it in a white scarf, the very same scarf she wrapped it in when she received it.

"Come on," says Ali. "Take it."

"Do we have a hiding place here?" asks Lisa.

"A very large one," Ali replies. "I've had fifteen people up there at one time." She looks at Lisa in alarm. "I'm not at my best today," she says, and sighs. "I'm dead tired, and I still have a lot to do. Would you please forget what I just said?"

"Fine," Lisa answers. "I've forgotten about those fifteen people and that you're dead tired."

"Who wants something to read?" Ali stands

up. "Here, I have all kinds of magazines for you. Who wants *Catholic Illustration*?"

"We all do," Lisa says.

"If you'll go upstairs to the hiding place and read quietly, I'll do the shopping. I'll make something good to eat. What shall it be? How about mashed potatoes with kale? Is that all right, children?"

"Yes," Eva replies.

"Mmm, delicious," Lisa answers.

"Then you'll go upstairs now. I'll be back in about an hour. Let me show you the hiding place. It's the safest one in Holland. I hope so, at least."

Ali is right about the hiding place; it is large, about the size of a small room. There are chairs, a bookcase full of books, and an electric light.

"We'll keep the light off for a while," says Papa. "It's a shame that we can only stay here for a couple of hours. It's amazing how Ali was able to make this room invisible."

The hiding place feels so safe that they almost forget they are in hiding. They sit and read, just as they used to do at home. Now and then they talk softly to one another.

"I'm hungry," says Lisa.

"Have a cookie," her mother jokes, taking a blue canister from the bookcase. She opens it. "I was right!" she exclaims, and laughs. "There really are cookies in here."

Papa looks at his watch. "It's five minutes to one," he announces.

"Isn't it taking Ali a long time to do the shopping?" Mama asks.

"Relax. It's not yet one o'clock," he says, glancing at his watch again. He puts his magazine down on the little table and looks at his watch once more.

"Something is wrong," Mama whispers.

Papa puts his finger to his lips. "The children," he says.

Eva smiles. How silly it is for Papa to say that. He must think that she and Lisa are still babies.

"Why are you smiling?" her mother asks.

"Never mind." Eva is serious once again.

"There's Ali," says Papa, and he takes a deep breath. "Listen."

They are silent. Ali will be coming upstairs now. She will slide open the door to the hiding place and say, "Come on, dinner is almost ready."

Nothing happens. The door remains closed. They hear men's voices in the hall downstairs.

The sound grows louder as the men climb the steps.

"You take the front door, van Dam, and I'll take the back. Then we'll go upstairs. That's where we'll get them."

"We're going to be caught," Lisa cries.

"Shh. Mouth shut," says Papa, and he takes Lisa's hand. Lisa takes Mama's hand, and Mama takes Eva's. They remain dead still. A door creaks nearby. There is a loud knock on a wall, then another knock, even louder.

"Nothing is behind here. It doesn't sound any different from the other walls," someone shouts.

"Did you see how that bitch ran on those big feet?" a man with a deep voice says. "She ran until she lost a shoe. That's when we grabbed her. We should have picked up her shoe too. This is the last room. If we don't find anyone here, we'll go get ourselves a drop. We deserve a stiff drink."

They hear the sound of footsteps, and the sound of curtains being opened, then closed again. A window is opened.

"There's no one on the roof either. We've taken these so-called resistance fighters off roofs too," they hear. "Comrade, there's no money to be earned here. Let's go. Forward, march!"

The sound of footsteps again, and laughter as well. A door slams shut.

"I want to leave. They'll be back. I know it for sure. Ali has been caught," says Lisa, and she shivers.

"I think it's horrible too, but we have no choice," says Papa. "In another couple of hours we'll have to leave. It will be dark then."

They sneak out of the house. Papa leads the way, with Mama and the children following. They must be careful not to run into anything in the dark. They walk down the Brinkstraat, pass the grocery store, and turn the corner.

A light is flickering in the corner window, enough to see what is displayed there: a cardboard sign with LOST AND FOUND printed in black letters. In front of the sign are five crumpled handkerchiefs, three wallets, and a stuffed toy monkey. Next to the little monkey is a shoe. It is turned over on its side, clearly revealing the shoe size, which is stamped upon the sole.

Size eleven.

Four Minus Two Is Two

"I'M MRS. OVERDEVEST. PLEASED TO MEET YOU."
The woman extends her hand. Her cheeks gleam
like polished apples.

"Dutour," says Papa. "Pleased to meet you."

"I'm Marie-Jeanne, and this is my sister, Marie-
Louise, and this is my mother, Mireille. We're
Huguenots," says Lisa, staring into the woman's face.

"Yes, yes," says the woman, and she smiles.
"Ali told me. She'll certainly be coming to see
you. Take your coats off, everyone, and we'll go
into the living room."

Eva looks at her father.

"I'm afraid that Ali won't be coming," he says.

"What do you mean? Why not?" Mrs.
Overdevest looks from the one to the other. "Is
something wrong?"

"Alas," says Papa, and he sighs.

"No!" Mrs. Overdevest sinks into a big chair. "Has she been caught? I spoke with her just a few hours ago. It can't be. Then why weren't you caught too?"

"We were sitting in a hiding place. We escaped by the back door as soon as it grew dark," he says. "They were convinced that there was no one left in the house."

"Who were 'they'?" asks Mrs. Overdevest, looking at Papa in disbelief.

"Dutch policemen. They searched the whole house but didn't find us."

"If Ali is tortured, she could betray us." The color has drained from the woman's cheeks. "Perhaps it would be better for you to leave. Here, take your coats."

"We don't know where to go. We haven't any other address." Mama's face is grim. "If we have to leave, I'm going to turn myself in to the Germans. I can't bear the strain any longer."

"Mireille!" Papa looks as though he wants to slap her. "Shut up. Be quiet, I tell you."

"I can't take it . . . I can't take it anymore. . . ."

Mrs. Overdevest walks to Mama and puts her arm around her shoulder. "Calm down," she whispers. "Calm down. I have an idea. I'll phone a woman named Henny and ask her to go to an address to see if they have room for you. Ali gave me Henny's number."

"We know Henny too," says Mama. "She works at the Municipal Hospital. She'll find a place for us."

Mrs. Overdevest leaves the room.

Lisa sits down on a wooden chair and buries her face in her hands. "Ali . . . it's so sad," she sobs. "Maybe they'll beat her with a whip. Maybe they'll beat her over the head and—"

"Quiet." Papa lifts her up and sits down in the chair. "Come up on my lap," he says softly. "I'm ninety-five percent certain that she won't squeal. Ali is so strong."

"What is ninety-five percent?" asks Lisa, wiping her nose on her sleeve. "I haven't had that in school yet. And what is 'squeal'?"

"You're smiling again, thank goodness. Ninety-five percent means almost certainly, and to squeal means to betray people, to tell the Germans something they shouldn't know, something that might put others in danger."

"Oh," says Lisa with a sigh. "Mama, *you* say something."

Mama is sitting with the basket on her lap. She is staring into space, just as she did at the bookstore.

Mrs. Overdevest returns to the room. "Henny will be coming in an hour," she says. "I'll give her the address I have in my head. Those people are sure to take you in."

"That's fine," says Papa.

Mama remains silent.

"Mireille," he whispers, and nudges her arm.

"Floor!" he shouts, calling her by her real name.

Mama looks up.

"Behave yourself," he says angrily. "I know it's been almost too much to bear today, but don't let me down, Floor."

"I'll do my best," Mama whispers.

"Would you like something to eat or drink?" Mrs. Overdevest asks.

"I don't," Eva replies. "My stomach is in knots."

"What would Ali be eating now?" Lisa asks.

The room is quiet. A clock that is wound by copper chains plays a little song every quarter of an hour. Henny arrives after the third song.

"It's just terrible about Ali," she says. "What

an awful shock. We have no time to lose. I'll go now and will return as fast as I can. No, I have a better idea. You never know. I'll take you with me. If Ali has been caught, then . . ."

"Good idea," says Mrs. Overdevest, and she turns to Papa. "You're in good hands with a girl who is wearing a nurse's uniform."

They have already put on their coats.

"Thank you," says Papa as he stands by the front door.

"You don't have to thank me," Mrs. Overdevest replies. "I hope that everything will be all right."

They walk through the dark streets. Henny turns on her flashlight every now and then; it makes a howling kind of sound whenever she pushes on the button.

"Where is *our* flashlight?" asks Mama. "Henny's flashlight reminds me of that thing all of a sudden."

They walk for about fifteen minutes, until they come to a large house. Henny pulls on the doorbell.

"Who's there?" asks a voice in the hall, right by the front door.

"It is I, and Ila sends her regards," Henny whispers through the mail slot.

There is the jingling of keys. The door opens.

"Come in," says a woman. "I'm Martha."

"And I'm Eduard," says a man who is standing behind her.

"My husband," says Martha. "I think I know why you're here. Are you seeking shelter?" She looks at her husband.

"Two can stay," he says. "We'll take the children. We don't have any of our own. It will be nice to have those two pretty girls. I really can't take in all four of you. My wife often helps out in a kindergarten. It would be too difficult to shelter an entire family."

"Then take the girls," says Henny. "I have another address, so that will be all right. Come on, say your good-byes, and we'll get going again."

They hug one another. "Good-bye, my dear, sweet Eva. We'll see each other soon." Papa takes her head between his hands. "Take care of your little sister."

He embraces Lisa. "Listen to your big sister," he says hoarsely.

Mama reaches into her pocket and pulls out two envelopes. "I have something for you," she says quietly. "It's a poem." She gives an envelope to each daughter. "They're both the same, in case the two of you are ever separated," she explains.

"We have to leave," says Henny.

"One more kiss," says Mama, and she wraps her arms around Eva.

Eva leans her head against her mother's shoulder. "Good-bye, Mama. Good-bye for now."

They kiss once more. They can hardly let go.

"We'll see each other again," says Papa. "Come, we have no choice. Good-bye for now. Here . . . the clown is for you. We don't need a mascot. Come on, we have to go."

Catching a final glimpse of their parents, the girls watch as Papa puts his arm around Mama's shoulder. Then Martha shuts the front door and locks it.

"Read the poem first," says Martha. "And my husband and I would like you to call us Aunt Martha and Uncle Eduard."

"That must be for safety's sake," exclaims Lisa. "And I'm your niece, of course, and my sister too, and we fled from Rotterdam after the bombing."

"That's right. You know the story very well," says Aunt Martha. "Read the poem. I'll prepare supper in the meantime. You must be hungry."

"Ali was going to make mashed potatoes with kale," says Lisa. "She's probably hungry too."

Eva opens her envelope after Aunt Martha has left the room. "Shall I read my poem out loud?" she asks. "You can read yours when I'm finished."

Eva begins:

"Dear Marie-Louise,
Our little boat is still afloat
Upon this great big sea of life,
God grant to us that we may live
In a world that's free of hate and strife,
And that you, my little girl, will find rest and
   peace,
That the wailing of sirens will someday cease
So that you may run and shout and play,
And stay outdoors the whole long day,
That we may be united, all,
In a house, however small,
And that in these terrible times, my dear,
You won't suffer too much, but be of good cheer,
Marie-Louise, you have a heart of gold,

Stay as sweet as you are, and do as you're told,
So that when the war has reached an end,
Everyone will want to be your friend,
May you always continue to thrive and grow,
These are words of your mother, who loves you so."

"I've looked at mine already," says Lisa. "It's the same poem as yours. And when the war is over, I'm going to cross out 'Marie-Jeanne' with thick black ink. And above this poem I'm going to write 'Dear Lisa Zilverstijn!!!' with three exclamation points."

"I have a cup of split pea soup for you!" Aunt Martha calls. "Come to the table!"

A New Cousin

EVA AND LISA HAVE BEEN LIVING UPSTAIRS AT Aunt Martha and Uncle Eduard's house for five weeks now. They've been terribly bored, but Aunt Martha has found something for them to do. One day she brought them a large skein of wool.

"First you must turn the skein into a nice ball of yarn, and then knit, girls. You'll start with socks, because they're the easiest."

She showed them how to wind the yarn. "Look, you hold your hands in front of you as if you want to tell how wide someone is. Then you make a ball by winding the yarn around your hands, beginning with the loose thread that you extract from the skein."

"Sooo . . . wide," Lisa said as she held her hands apart. "It's just like a flower wreath, except it's made of wool." That was exactly how Aunt Martha had meant for it to be.

"Good for you," she exclaimed. "You can get to work now."

The girls have become champion sock knitters, with four needles too. At first they thought knitting was fun, but they don't like it at all anymore. Their hands are sore, and Eva has developed a stiff neck as well.

"I don't want to knit socks anymore," she complained to Aunt Martha, but Aunt Martha wouldn't let her stop.

"You must keep yourself occupied; otherwise you'll fall asleep, and that's not good for children," she said. "Children must be kept busy."

Aunt Martha is right. When they can't think of any more games to play, and when there is absolutely nothing left for them to do, they fall asleep . . . just like that.

Just as Lisa has fallen asleep now.

Eva is sitting at the table with her hands clasped behind her head. She is gazing up and staring at the chubby angels that are carved in the ceiling.

One angel begins to move. "Hello, Eva," he says. "How are you?"

"I'm all right."

"You're fibbing," the little angel replies. "You miss your father and mother."

"No, I don't. I knit all the time."

"I can see that. I can see everything. But you still miss your parents."

Eva unclasps her hands and bows her head.

"Keep looking at me," says the angel. "Do you want to know my name?"

"No."

"My name is Emanuel."

"That's almost the same as Davy and Doortje's father. His name is Samuel."

"Would you like to go see them?"

"Yes."

"Well, I can't help you. I'm stuck here, just like you."

Other angels are beginning to move now. "Whom are you talking with, Emanuel?" asks one.

"With Eva Zilverstijn," he answers. "We must help her a little bit. She's having a hard time." His voice drops to a whisper. "She's Jewish, you see."

"Keep your mouth shut," Eva says aloud.

"I *am* keeping my mouth shut. I'm not saying anything," says Lisa, and she looks at her sister. "I really didn't say anything. You must have been dreaming."

"There on the ceiling . . . those angels."

"We see them every day," says Lisa. "What about them?"

Eva looks up again. Emanuel is silent.

"Let's take a walk," Lisa whispers. "Just as we did yesterday, remember? We'll go skating again and drink aniseed milk. When we imagined it yesterday, it seemed so real that I felt cold when we skated and warm when we were inside again. Remember?"

"Let's get back to our knitting," says Eva.

"Bah," Lisa grumbles.

Yesterday, when they were not yet finished taking their imaginary walk, Aunt Martha came upstairs and sat with them at the table. She doesn't do that very often.

"Fine, you have another sock for me," she said, and picked up the sock that Lisa had just finished.

"In a couple of days you won't have so much time to knit anymore," Aunt Martha blurted out suddenly.

"Do we have to leave?" Eva's heart began to beat so fast that it felt as though it would jump right out of her chest.

"No, definitely not." Aunt Martha looked secretively from Eva to Lisa. "Tomorrow a girl will be coming to stay, a cousin of yours."

"A cousin of ours?" said Lisa, almost falling from her chair. "We don't have any cousins who are girls. They're all boys: Robbie, Hans, and little Heiman. And I think that all those cousins have been sent to Westerbork."

"Listen," said Aunt Martha, and she coughed. "I have a sister and brother-in-law who have eleven children. Trijntje is the youngest. My sister is quite ill, so Trijntje will be staying with us for a while. Eduard and I are your uncle and aunt. That makes Trijntje your cousin."

"Oh, is that how it works?" asked Lisa. "When is she coming?"

"I said tomorrow, didn't I?"

Trijntje has been in the house for a couple of days now. She is big and fat and has fire red cheeks, just like Aunt Martha. She has promised her aunt and uncle that she will never, ever tell anyone about the two Jewish children upstairs.

"You must give me your word of honor. And a word of honor is something holy," Aunt Martha told Trijntje.

"Just as holy as the saints in the *Catholic Illustration* that we read at Ali's house?" Lisa asked.

"*Much* holier," replied Aunt Martha, looking very serious.

Trijntje herself is not holy. She does mean things.

"Do you know why I'm allowed to get up earlier than you?" she said this morning. "Because I get to have bread with bacon, and you don't."

"We're not allowed to eat bacon, you idiot," said Lisa. "God won't let us. We're not Catholic."

"I know. You're . . . you're . . . It wasn't bacon anyway. I was mistaken. It was bread with chocolate sprinkles."

Eva and Lisa remained silent.

"Ignore her," said Eva when Trijntje had gone back downstairs again. "I think she's lying through her teeth."

"Maybe if I play with you a lot, I won't have to go to school here," says Trijntje. "I do want to go to school, but not until my mother is better. And I want to be with my own class, not in a class here in Enschede. What shall we do?"

"Let's play dreamer," says Lisa.

"Dreamer?" Trijntje brings her face close to Lisa's. "What kind of stupid game is that? It must be a . . . um . . . Jewish game."

"No, *everyone* knows this game," Lisa answers. "You make up a dream, and you begin to tell it. After a while you point to someone else and say, 'Your turn,' and whoever you've pointed to has to continue. But you have to tell enough of the dream before you point to the next person."

"I'll begin," says Eva. "I'm dreaming . . . I'm dreaming . . . about a house with a garden. Beautiful flowers are blooming: East Indian cherry, hydrangeas, and a laburnum tree with golden blossoms. When it rains, the children who live in the house go outside and catch golden raindrops. 'Look, gold,' they shout. They bring out huge buckets in order to collect the golden rain. Your turn, Lisa."

"When the storm is over, the children bring the golden raindrops inside," Lisa continues. "And then a grown-up comes and says, 'What do you have there?' 'Golden raindrops,' answer the children. 'Throw them in the garden!' the grown-up screams. 'It's poison . . . the golden rain is poison!' The children—Your turn, Trijntje. You finish the dream."

"The children don't listen to the grown-up," says Trijntje. "They drink the golden rain. At first nothing happens, but then they all drop dead. Except for one, who has listened to the grown-up and hasn't drunk any of the golden rain. And that one child gets to live with the grown-up all by herself, but first all the poisoned children have to be buried under the laburnum tree. And the child and the grown-up live happily ever after."

"That was good," says Lisa.

"It was weird, but good," Eva comments.

"Trijntje, come downstairs!" calls Aunt Martha.

Trijntje doesn't hear her. "Shall we play another game?" she asks. "Shall we play dreamer again?"

"I'll start," says Lisa. "There was once a girl who had a mother. That mother would just give her children away, because she had eleven of them. One day she said to the youngest, 'You're my least favorite child of all, so I'll be giving you—'"

"I'm going to eat," says Trijntje. "I get to go downstairs and you—"

"Get lost!" Lisa shouts. "And be quick about it!"

Jan and Annie

"What are we going to do tomorrow, Eva?"

The girls are lying in bed together. Lisa crawls close to her sister. "Come on, Eva. Answer me. What are we doing tomorrow?"

"The same thing as yesterday and the day before yesterday and last week. Knit socks for the poor children at Aunt Martha's school," Eva would like to say, but she doesn't. She doesn't want to make Lisa unhappy.

"Tomorrow we'll go to school, just like Trijntje," she whispers. "We'll go outside, just like that. Then we'll visit Grandpa and Grandma, because the Germans haven't arrested them yet, and they're still living in their house. We'll drink punch through a straw, and Grandma will tell us about the time when she was young and still living in Germany. Of course she's learned to speak Dutch by now."

"Don't be silly, Eva!" exclaims Lisa, and she moves to the edge of the bed. "You shouldn't tell lies like that. You know it's not true."

"I like to pretend that we're living in the past," Eva whispers. "Shall we go to sleep now?"

Lisa snuggles up to her again. "All right," she answers. "See you in the morning."

"See you in the morning," says Eva, and she tries to curl up like a little dog. She wants very much to sleep, but Lisa is lying so close to her that she can't. She begins to think about the past. It is as though a movie is being played in her head, a movie that takes place in Rotterdam. Once again she is living next door to Ali's sister, Mrs. Terhegge. Lodewijk is there too, Mrs. Terhegge's crazy parrot that cries, "Dirty bastard," whenever it hears Hitler's name mentioned.

She feels a hard nudge against her side.

"Why are you calling out, 'Hitler,' Eva? I can't sleep when you do that. That stupid Hitler wants to send us to Westerbork."

Lisa sits up in bed. "My head itches," she says.

She bends forward and shakes her head. "No, no, no!" she shouts, scratching her head with both hands. "It's driving me crazy."

"Shall I blow on your head?" Eva asks. "It will make you feel cooler, and you won't itch so much."

She blows as hard as she can. It helps a bit at first, but Lisa soon begins to scratch again.

"Come on, move your hands away," says Eva. She takes a strand of Lisa's hair and examines it. "There's nothing to see," she says. "Oh-oh, there's one, and there's another one."

"Again?" Lisa looks very unhappy all of a sudden. "Aunt Martha said that she'll cut our hair off if it happens again. And I don't want to be bald."

"We won't tell her. We won't scratch whenever Aunt Martha is near," says Eva. "Silly Lisa, you've shaken them onto my head. Now *I* itch too."

The girls sit next to each other and lean against their pillows.

"We both have head lice again," says Eva with a sigh. "Those filthy things will eat our hair all up, and when they're finished, they'll eat *us* up too. We'll be gone then and won't have to be in hiding anymore."

"Don't say that, Eva. I wish we were with Papa and Mama and that we were all at home together, just as we were before Hitler came along. Our own father and mother wouldn't shave us bald. Do you remember what they look like?"

Eva thinks deeply before answering. "Mama is blond, and she has blue eyes. And Papa is a little bit bald, with brown eyes."

"Yes, I know, but I think that their actual photo that I've kept in my head has been gobbled up by the lice," says Lisa. "Mama and Papa would take those lice and shoot them dead, every last one of them. Right, Eva?"

The very thought of their parents taking a shotgun to their head lice makes the girls laugh so loudly that they must go under the covers. If Aunt Martha were to hear such a commotion, she would separate them. Eva would then have to sleep on a mattress in the attic, under the long white underpants that are hanging on the clothesline and among the potatoes, which have little white worms crawling out of them.

Eva and Lisa know they're not allowed to get up yet, even though it is already eight o'clock. Each morning as they lie in bed, they remain dead still in order to listen to the sounds that rise up through the floor. They can hear Trijntje laughing, the teakettle whistling, and Uncle Eduard's deep voice. When the front door slams shut, they know that Trijntje has left for school. When Uncle Eduard takes his bicycle out, the door to the shed creaks twice: once when it is opened and again when it is closed.

This morning they must wait a very long time for Aunt Martha to tell them they're allowed to get up.

"Oh . . . there they are again!" Lisa throws off the covers and begins to scratch. She is sitting on the white sheet with her legs apart and her head bowed. "Look!" she shouts. "I see one over to the right, near my knee."

"Shh!" Eva puts her hand over her sister's mouth. "Don't shout like that. Aunt Martha and your bald head, remember?"

"Actually, it's kind of cute with all those legs," says Lisa, more quietly this time. "You try to catch one, Eva."

Eva bows her head and searches wildly through her hair. "Yes!" she says, giggling. "Look. This gray louse is mine."

"Mine is faster," says Lisa, and begins to laugh so hard that she must pull a blanket over her head. When she has stopped, she takes the blanket away.

"Shall we race them?" she asks. "Or put them in a circus? There really is such a thing as a flea circus. Let's create a louse circus. I'll be a louse tamer." Lisa pulls a hair from her head. "Jump over this hair, you louse," she commands with a giggle. "Hoopla!"

"I'd rather have a race," says Eva.

"All right. We'll start together." Lisa begins to count. "One, two, three. What's the name of your louse?"

"That gray one's name is . . ." Eva must think for a minute. "His name is . . . Chaïm Goldman."

"It can't be that. Jewish names aren't allowed. It's too dangerous. We haven't kept *our* own names, have we? Our name isn't Zilverstijn anymore."

"Then I'll name mine Jan."

"And I'll name mine Annie. Come, Annie," says Lisa, and she picks up the louse that is almost at the foot of the bed.

Eva picks up the gray one.

"I'll count again: One, two, three, go!" Lisa

gives it a little push. "Mine has won!" she cries.

"No, *mine* has won," Eva shouts. "Jan is the winner!"

"What are you doing?" Aunt Martha is standing in the doorway. "Are you crazy? You're making much too much noise. Do you want to be caught and sent to a concentration camp?"

"No," Lisa replies. "Our grandpa and grandma are already in a camp, but we don't want to go to one, do we, Eva?"

"Don't let me hear you shouting like that again."

"No, Aunt Martha," the girls answer in unison.

"If you're going to make such a racket, I'll have to find another address for you. Do you want me to do that?"

"No, Aunt Martha," they answer again.

"I have some very unpleasant news about Trijntje," says Aunt Martha, and she sighs. "This morning I saw that she has head lice. I think she caught those disgusting things at school. Tonight I'll put kerosene in her hair. She'll have to sleep with a towel wrapped around her head."

"Will you have to shave her hair off if the

kerosene doesn't work?" asks Eva. She can't help smiling a little.

"Of course not," says Aunt Martha. "You can't do that to a child who goes to school. It would be different with you and Marie-Jeanne because you can't leave the house. But luckily I haven't seen you girls scratching lately."

"No," says Lisa. "My head doesn't itch at all. We don't have head lice. We have only Jan and Annie."

Eva begins to choke with laughter.

"You two are getting stranger and stranger," Aunt Martha exclaims. "Who on earth are Jan and Annie?"

"They're friends from Trijntje's school," says Eva. "They spend the whole day with us."

Aunt Martha stands by the bed. "Come," she says. "It's time to get up. I'll be back in a little while with your breakfast. Then I'll give you some new yarn. I want a sock from each of you today. Now get dressed." She pulls the covers away. "Come on, get up!"

"Watch out!" Lisa cries. "Watch out for Jan and Annie!"

"Shh. Not so loud, Marie-Jeanne. Won't you ever learn?" Aunt Martha leaves the room, shaking her head in disapproval.

"That's what happens to children who've been locked up for such a long time," the girls hear her say. "They become completely crazy."

Eva and Lisa burst out laughing. They must pull the covers over their heads once again.

But where are Jan and Annie?

YELLOW

"COME DOWNSTAIRS WITH ME FOR A LITTLE while," says Aunt Martha. "Come on. Don't be afraid. I've already closed the curtains. It's a shame that Trijntje is spending the day with her parents, isn't it? You'll be bored now."

"Oh, we don't mind . . . ouch! Don't kick, Eva."

"I'm not doing anything," Eva says sharply.

The girls tiptoe down the stairs. They skip over the second and tenth steps because they creak so loudly.

"You must stay upstairs and be as quiet as newborn mice," Aunt Martha told Eva and Lisa upon their arrival. "When Uncle Eduard and I aren't here, no one is to know that there are other people in the house."

In spite of the warning, they secretly went downstairs one morning, when Aunt Martha was helping at her school. That is how they know about the creaking of the steps.

While the girls are upstairs, they whisper about the past, when they were still living at home with their parents and were free to sleep over at friends' houses.

"Eva, remember when the curtains could stay open when we were in the room?"

Lisa often asks such questions, and Eva finds them tiresome. She doesn't want to think so much about the past. She would prefer to think about Aunt Martha and her school and about the children whom Aunt Martha has claimed as her own.

"You two sit over there." Aunt Martha points to a red plush sofa. "I'll sit across from you."

She smooths out her dress and sighs deeply. "I'm afraid I have some bad news to tell you," she says quietly.

"Papa and Mama have been caught," says Lisa. "I can feel it."

"No, it's not that, thank goodness. But your mother is very sick. She has jaundice. Her whole body is yellow."

"As yellow as the star we used to wear on our clothes?"

"Even yellower, Lisa. She's as yellow as—" Aunt Martha's eyes shift toward the painting that hangs above the sofa. "As yellow as those lemons," she says.

Eva and Lisa turn around to look.

"The star was much yellower than those lemons, and I want to go see her," exclaims Lisa. "Right away."

Aunt Martha stands up and walks to the sofa. "Sweetheart, you *can't*. You know that, don't you?"

She looks at Eva. "You're the eldest. You know that's impossible, don't you? It's much too dangerous. You could be caught, and I could be caught too."

"You don't have to come with us," says Eva. "I know where our parents are. You walk down the street and turn the corner. They're at Piet van Proosdij's house, and it has a blue roof and—"

"How do *you* know?" Aunt Martha's cheeks are even redder than usual. She grabs Eva by the shoulders and shakes her back and forth. "Speak up. How do you know that? If you're caught, you'll give everything away. I'm sure of that."

Eva presses her lips together. She will never tell anyone how she picked up that information. She won't even tell the Nazis if they should come and arrest her.

"Upstairs with you, you stubborn girl," Aunt Martha commands. "Marie-Jeanne may stay down here for a bit."

"I'm going upstairs too." Lisa follows her sister. "And I still want to see my mama."

They are lying in bed, hand in hand. They can't sleep.

"Shall we go now, Eva? Aunt Martha won't hear anything. She cares only about her children at school. Why won't you answer? Are you crying? Then I'll cry with you."

Eva does her best to cry silently, but she can't. "Mama is going to die," she sobs. "Dead people are yellow too."

"Maybe she's turned yellow from being inside," says Lisa, trying to comfort her. "What are you doing now? Stop!"

Lisa jumps out of bed. "You're disgusting. You've thrown up all over me. I'm going to wake Aunt Martha."

Eva hears the steps creaking as Lisa walks downstairs.

"Mama!" she cries.

"Are you that unhappy, sweetheart? I didn't know that you would take it so hard."

Aunt Martha is sitting on the edge of the bed, despite the filth. "I'm sorry, I'm sorry that I was so nasty to you. I should have known better, but the stress was too much for me, you see."

"It doesn't matter," says Eva. "I'm all right now. And the reason I know where Papa and Mama are is because whenever Henny comes over, I sit on the stairs and listen to you talk."

"It's sweet of you to tell me that now. Shall we . . . shall we go see your parents?"

"Yes, yes, yes!" Lisa shouts.

"Shh." Aunt Martha puts a finger to her lips. "Not so loud, Marie-Jeanne. We'll go tomorrow night."

"Will there be a moon then?" asks Eva.

"It will be dark," Aunt Martha says.

The girls have decided to bundle the clown in the white scarf and take it with them, along with three apples for Mama and two for Papa. Aunt Martha picked them before she left for school this morning. She took a red apple and polished it on her red-checked skirt.

"Pretty, isn't it?" she exclaimed. "And now I'm going to school." She locked the outside door and was gone.

"Eva, what do you think?" Lisa asks. "What will they say when we're standing right in front of their very eyes all of a sudden?"

"Maybe they won't recognize us," Eva replies.

"They'll recognize *me*," says Lisa. "I still have the same pigtails as before. Shall we read Mama's poem again? The day will pass more quickly then. We'll take turns and read it line by line. I'll begin:

"Our little boat is still afloat
Upon this great big sea of life,
God grant to us—"

"Stop," says Eva, and she sighs. "God won't grant anything to us. He won't grant us anything at all."

"But don't you think the poem is beautiful?" asks Lisa. "I want to write poetry like that when I'm a mother. What shall we do now?"

"Sleep," says Eva. She crawls into bed, pulls the covers over her head, and is silent.

"I'm getting into bed too," Lisa whispers. "Tonight we're going to see our yellow mama, and I'm going to give her two million kisses."

The time has come. The girls are standing in the hallway, ready to leave. Lisa is holding the picture of the clown.

"Maybe *he* can make Mama better," Eva said this afternoon.

Aunt Martha brought their coats from the attic. Eva and Lisa think it's strange to be wearing coats again. The coats feel a bit tight.

"We'll take the path that runs along the back gardens," Aunt Martha says.

"That's the same way we walked when Ali took us to a new address," Lisa whispers.

"Remember, keep looking at the ground and don't say a word. If someone should talk to you, don't answer. I'll do that for you. Come, let's go." Aunt Martha gives each of them a little push. "Come on. You *do* want to go, don't you?"

With heads bowed they walk down the path. They see the gray cobblestones moving beneath their feet. They pass over more cobblestones as they walk faster and faster.

"Here it is. Don't be frightened. The gate creaks a little," says Aunt Martha, and she opens it.

They tiptoe through a garden and approach a door. Aunt Martha taps three times.

A big man opens the door partway. A light is shining behind him.

It is Piet van Proosdij! The girls know it for sure.

"They've come to see their mother," whispers Aunt Martha.

"Wait here for a minute." The man opens the door all the way.

They walk through and find themselves standing in a shed. It contains a large wooden washing machine and rakes and brooms, which are hanging on the wall.

The man returns. "Their mother is contagious," he says. "They mustn't get near her."

"We have a painting for her and five apples. Two for Papa and three for Mama," says Lisa. "We want to give this to them ourselves."

"You can't," says the man. "Much too dangerous. Give these things to me."

"Can't they even see their father?" Aunt Martha inquires. "Ask him to come down."

"I'd better not. That man couldn't handle it." Piet van Proosdij holds the door open for them.

"Go now," he says. "I won't tell them that you were here. Much too sad for those Jews upstairs. Adieu!"

"You're a mean liar!" Eva would like to scream at him. "My parents have been caught, and you act as though they're upstairs."

"Come," says Aunt Martha. "Let's go home."

"I'm not going!" Eva shouts.

"Shh!" Aunt Martha puts her hand over Eva's mouth. "Behave yourself," she hisses. "If anyone sees us, we'll be caught."

"Fine. At least I'd be with my father and mother again."

"I don't want to be caught." Lisa begins to weep.

"I don't either." Eva weeps too.

Later, when they are back at Aunt Martha's house, Eva will crawl into bed. She will pull the covers over her head and sleep until the war is over.

Perhaps she will have to sleep for a hundred years.

ITCH

"SHALL I TELL YOU A BIG SECRET?" TRIJNTJE whispers. "Henny is coming tonight, and she has something important to say, but I don't know what. And I have another secret. Do you want to hear it?"

"Yes."

"Do you know why I don't sleep in the same room as you? It's because I'm allowed to get up before you are, and then I get to play with the toys that Aunt Martha played with when she was young, and you don't."

"And Aunt Martha makes *you* go to school, and *we* don't have to," says Eva. She sticks out her tongue. "Too bad. *We* get to stay inside all the time."

"I also get to eat candied sugar and porridge without lumps and . . ." Trijntje begins to scratch.

"This itch is driving me crazy," she complains.

"Do you have fleas?" Eva inquires.

"Or lice perhaps?" says Lisa.

"No, look." Trijntje spreads her fingers. "Take a look at all the little bumps. And here too." She pushes up her sleeve. "I have all these little bumps on my elbow."

"Bah, how nasty. You should tell Aunt Martha," says Eva, shivering. "Maybe you'll have to put kerosene on them."

"Nasty? I think it's nice." Lisa cheers. "The Nazis are scared to death of you when you've got bumps or spots on your body. If the Nazis were to come and find us all broken out like that, they wouldn't take us with them."

"Shut up," Eva snaps. "Don't say such rotten things. You're giving me a stomachache."

"Trijntje has scabies," says Aunt Martha. "I sent her to the doctor. She has an ointment that must be applied to her whole body. It's a good thing that you don't sleep in the same room with her because scabies is contagious."

"I hope your children at school don't get it," Eva remarks.

"And I hope *you* don't get it either," says Aunt

Martha with a sigh. "Three children with scabies would be too much for me."

"Why is Henny coming tonight?"

"What do you mean, Marie-Louise?"

"Trijntje said—"

"Is she doing it again? Has she been gossiping again? She'll have to go home if this continues. What are you doing, Marie-Louise?"

"Nothing. Nothing at all."

"You're scratching."

"Yes."

"Let me see." Aunt Martha rolls up Eva's sleeve. "Oh, no!" she cries. "Another one. Does it itch?"

"Yes, a whole lot." Eva begins to scratch everywhere.

"I'll have to smear the ointment on you too," Aunt Martha wails. "And pretty soon Marie-Jeanne will be coming down with it as well. It's too much for me. I'll have to discuss the situation with Uncle Eduard."

"Let me see," says Henny. "I want to see your whole body. I know what scabies looks like because there have been cases of it at the hospital. Take off your clothes."

Eva and Lisa stand in front of Henny, stark naked.

"When do you itch the most, Marie-Louise?"

"In bed," Lisa answers. "At night she scratches herself silly. And I'm starting to get it too. Here, under my arms." She raises both arms up high.

"Indeed," says Henny, and sighs. "You have scabies, all three of you. You need to be treated with Scabinol."

"Will we have to go away now?" Eva inquires. "What do you think, Henny?"

"It would be easier for Martha if I could come each evening and put the ointment on you. Unfortunately that's impossible."

"Why is it impossible?"

"I'll explain, Marie-Louise. But first put your clothes back on."

"And *I* want to go home," says Trijntje. "Aunt Martha thinks I'm a chatterbox because I said that you'd be coming this evening."

"So, we're dressed." Eva pulls her sweater over her head. "Tell us why it's impossible to come and put that smelly ointment. . . . You look sad, Henny. Does the ointment have something to do with it?"

"Yes." Henny takes a handkerchief from the pocket of her apron. "I'm sad because my coming here so often is getting to be too dangerous for us all."

"But don't you often go and see Davy and Doortje?"

"What—what did you say, Marie-Louise?"

"Don't you often visit Davy and Doortje?"

"Uh, no—yes, indeed I do. I—"

"Where are Davy and Doortje? They've been caught, I can feel it. You're lying!"

"Shh. Not so loud, Marie-Louise."

"Where are they? Have they been caught?" asks Eva, more quietly this time. "It's not true, is it? Tell me I'm wrong. Please, Henny!"

Henny shakes her head. "Alas, you are right. I didn't want you to know anything about this. Grandpa and Geesje and the Baruch family—all betrayed and arrested." She sighs deeply. "Terrible, isn't it?"

"Maybe they'll see Omi Schillaj again," says Lisa. "Maybe they're all together in Westerbork now."

"I'm afraid they're not." Henny does not look at her.

"Then where is Omi Schillaj?" asks Eva.

"She was sent farther on, to Poland," Henny replies. She puts her hands over her eyes. "I couldn't warn them . . . too late . . . too late . . . I had wanted to say that. . . . "

"And what about the hiding place where we often played together?"

"That's probably where they were, Marie-Louise. Very likely they heard the Sicherheits-dienst enter the house. Their neighbor, Mrs. Verwey, told me that she watched as they were taken outside, all six of them. One SDer walked in front, and another walked in back, next to Grandpa. He said something very cruel to Grandpa. 'You thought that we had already left, old man, didn't you? Wrong! We were sitting at the table in the attic, and we were dead silent, just like fishermen waiting to catch a fish. And after fifteen minutes . . . that's right, we got you! You shouldn't have coughed, man.'"

Henny sighs. "Mrs. Verwey could understand everything because she speaks German," she says.

"Do you know what I want more than anything else in the world?" Lisa looks from one to the other.

"No. What is it?" Henny takes her by the hand. "It's all right to tell us."

"I want—I want—I don't really know what I want. Yes, I do. I want everyone to be free again, and I want the war to end, and I want the scabies to disappear, and the SDers too. And I want to stop being so afraid."

"Me too," says Henny very quietly. "God, child, how right you are. For I'm often afraid."

Eva puts her fingers in her ears. "Quiet," she says. "Don't say things like that."

"I'm sorry." Henny stands and smooths her apron. "But I'm only human. I'm just an ordinary human being."

"No, you're not." Lisa stands up too and wraps her arms around her. "You are a hero!" she exclaims. "And Davy and Doortje will be coming back, because we promised to stay together forever. When we were at Geesje's house, we held hands and made a pledge that the four of us—"

"Don't talk about it." Henny pats Lisa on the shoulder. "But keep believing in magic, Marie-Jeanne. Please, keep believing that they'll be coming back."

Parcheesi

Trijntje continues to be a nuisance. She pretends to be very nice whenever Aunt Martha and Uncle Eduard are around, but she says the most vicious things when she is alone with Eva and Lisa: "If you don't give me a piece of your apple, I'm going to tell my teacher that you're here. And Mr. Verheul is in the Nazi party. He's an NSBer." And: "If you don't let me win this card game, I'll go to the police."

Usually they don't answer, but last week Eva couldn't keep it in any longer. "Idiot, then you and Uncle Eduard and Aunt Martha will be arrested too!" she cried, and stuck out her tongue.

Lisa didn't say anything at first, but when she saw how frightened Trijntje became, she dared to speak up as well. "Then you'll be sent to a work camp, and you'll have to work very hard," she said. "You'll have to—Eva, what did you say she'd have to do?"

"Cut down trees," Eva answered. "With a big rusty saw, all by herself. And if she cuts her finger, she'll get blood poisoning and die."

Trijntje turned bright red. "I'm going to tell my aunt that you're being mean to me," she shouted. "Then you'll have to get the hell out of here, and I'll have Aunt Martha all to myself." She stormed out of the room and slammed the door behind her.

"You dirty, rotten girl, wait till I get my hands on you!" Lisa yelled at the closed door. "I'll—I'll—"

"Never mind," said Eva, giggling. "She's scared stiff. If she gets nasty again, we'll just make up something else to tell her."

"We'll give her two black eyes," Lisa whispered. She reflected for a moment. "Eva, do you remember the song about the eyes? The eyes in the song aren't black, though; they're blue."

"Two eyes so blue, two eyes so blue,
I love those peepers of yours, I do,
Two eyes so blue."

They sang the song again, until Lisa stopped all of a sudden.

"Why don't you keep singing, Lisa? It's such a nice song."

"But it's Mama's song. Remember?"

"Don't be silly," Eva answered a bit angrily. "Of course I remember. When we were at home she always sang that song for us, in her own language. I think it was the language from Groningen. And together we'd sit in Mama's lap, and she would rock us back and forth while she sang."

For a long time the girls sat on the bed without saying a word. Finally Lisa dared to speak. "I miss Papa and Mama *so* much, Eva. Do you miss them too?"

They tried to keep the tears from coming, but it was no use. They wept a little, until Lisa stopped and spoke again.

"I'm all right now," she stated, and tried to smile through her tears.

"I am too," Eva blubbered. "But I don't want to hear that song until we're back home again."

Aunt Martha and Trijntje will not be going out today, even though it is Wednesday. The heater at

Aunt Martha's school is broken, and Trijntje is sick. She has a sore throat, and a dirty yellow discharge is oozing from her eyes.

It is too cold for Trijntje upstairs; therefore Eva and Lisa are allowed to come downstairs and play cards and Parcheesi with her. They are sitting at the round table in the kitchen, under the paraffin lamp.

Aunt Martha has shut the curtains. "It's safer that way, for no one can see you," she explains. "The neighbors won't think there's anything unusual about the curtains because it's a dark day anyway. But we do have to make arrangements beforehand, in case something should happen."

She points to Eva and Lisa. "If the doorbell rings, you girls will run upstairs. And, Trijntje, you will put the cards and the games back in the cupboard. Understand?"

The three girls nod.

"We had to do the same thing at Geesje's house a couple of addresses ago," says Lisa.

Aunt Martha looks directly at Trijntje. "And you may never, ever open the door when they're downstairs," she says, and points to Eva and Lisa. "Understand, Trijntje?"

Trijntje nods.

It is nice and warm in the kitchen. A lamp is burning, the teakettle is hissing on the stove, and a big clock is ticking. The die rolls on the table, and pawns tap against the board.

"It's just like peacetime," Lisa exclaims as they drink hot chocolate.

"Six!" Trijntje calls. "I'm almost in!"

"No, you're not." Eva picks up the die. "Look, it's a four."

"If you don't let me win, I'll . . ." Trijntje looks at Lisa.

Lisa sticks out her tongue. Eva kicks her sister in the shin.

"Ouch. Stop!"

Suddenly there is a sharp, rapping sound on the windowpane.

"Quick!" calls Aunt Martha. "Aafje Bezemer taps her ring against the kitchen window whenever she comes over. Get upstairs!"

Trijntje pushes Eva and Lisa to the steps. "Run!" she says.

Breathlessly they fall onto their bed. "I'm scared!" Lisa exclaims, panting.

"Shh. Don't be scared."

The girls sit next to each other without saying a word. They can hear Trijntje's voice and another voice as well.

"Aunt Martha let someone in," whispers Lisa. "Listen. I hear a girl. Maybe they're playing Parcheesi."

"I think you're right," says Eva, sliding off the bed. She puts her ear to the floor and listens.

She hears the tapping of pawns against the game board.

"Four!" the visitor calls.

"Six!" shouts Trijntje.

"I'll go make some pancakes," they hear Aunt Martha say.

"I hope the pancakes are all burned," Lisa whispers. "I hope they turn out pitch black."

Later that week, when Trijntje is feeling better, she tells the girls that Aafje Bezemer has spread a rumor to all the neighbors.

"'There's something funny going on at Martha and Eduard's house,' she said to everyone. 'There must be people in hiding there. They often keep the curtains closed, even during the daytime.' Then someone from the underground came to her and said he'd shoot her if she didn't stop spreading such rumors," Trijntje reports.

"Liar!" exclaims Lisa. "What a liar you are!"

"No, I'm not," Trijntje answers. "And *I* get to go home now, to my own father and mother. They think it's too dangerous for me here."

She looks from Eva to Lisa. "And *you* won't be going back to *your* parents for a long time."

"Go on home," Lisa snarls. "Your father and mother will get scabies then, and your brothers and sisters too. All thirteen of you will stink like Scabinol."

Trijntje walks slowly out of the room. Her back is as straight as an arrow.

Eva slams the door behind her. "So Trijntje is going home," she says. "Good riddance."

GUESTS

"WE'RE HAVING COMPANY TONIGHT," AUNT
Martha announces. "People from Eduard's
factory will be coming over. You'll have to be
quieter than usual, but I can't tell you anything
more about it for the time being."

"Is it your birthday?" Lisa asks.

"I told you that I wouldn't say anything
more, didn't I?" exclaims Aunt Martha. She takes
a cigarette from an elegant little box that has the
word *Kyriazi* printed upon it. She lights the
cigarette, inhales deeply, and blows a white cloud
of smoke into the room.

"I'll tell you once again . . . remember, not a
sound out of you tonight," she tells them sternly.
She stands up and stretches. "All right, I'll be
going now."

The girls can smell the cigarette long after Aunt Martha has left.

"We should give her a birthday present, but we don't have anything," says Eva.

"Then I'll go shopping. Where is my coat?" asks Lisa. She walks to a shiny brown wardrobe. "Here it is!" she exclaims, and dances a bit before putting the coat on. "My coat is much too small. What am I going to do when we go outside again?"

"You'll have to go without a coat," says Eva. "Take it off now."

"No, I'm keeping it on because I'm going to buy something for Aunt Martha."

"Take your coat off. We can't go outside."

"I know it. I'm going to pretend to buy something." Lisa walks a few steps and stops in front of a little table.

"Sir," she says in a high voice. "You, sir, behind the table. I'd like a beautiful blue vase. Do you have one in stock?

"Of course, my girl," Lisa answers in a deep voice. "What size vase would you like?"

Lisa stoops down and points from the floor to her navel. "So big," she squeaks, and reaches into her coat pocket. "I have ten guilders. Is that enough?

"Yes," she growls in the salesclerk's voice. "Whom is this vase for?

"For Aunt Martha. It's her birthday. We're taking the tram to her house because she lives a little bit far from us. We're going during the daytime, and without a star too. We'll get to eat whipped-cream cake.

"Here is the vase, my girl. What's your name?

"Marie-Jeanne Dutour and Lisa Zilverstijn.

"Hmm. How silly it is to have so many names. I have only two. One first name and one last name.

"Then you certainly must not be Jewish, sir.

"No, thank goodness."

"Stop it. You're much too loud." Eva pulls on Lisa's sleeve. "Go sit down."

"Oh, look at that. Aunt Martha's vase is broken. It's your fault."

Eva touches Lisa's cheek with her finger. "How did you do that?" she asks.

"How did I get these tears? I don't know. They just came, that's all. I didn't do anything." Lisa puts a finger in each corner of her mouth and pulls tightly. "Look, I'm smiling again," she says.

■ ■ ■

They ate supper earlier than usual: soup, brown beans, and applesauce.

"Go to sleep early," advised Aunt Martha. "Then I'll be sure that you won't make any noise. I can't have it any other way, I'm afraid."

That is why Eva and Lisa are lying in bed, even though it is only seven o'clock. They have already exhausted the games that can be played in a whisper: I spy and rhyming games. They will have to stop now because they have run out of things to do.

"It's seven-thirty," Lisa whispers. "I hear the church clock. I have to go to the bathroom."

"Then go quickly. Soon you won't be able to because the company will be here."

It is so quiet that Eva can hear her sister using the toilet. There is the sound of heavy footsteps in the hall downstairs. That must be Uncle Eduard.

"Welcome!" he calls. He says something else, but Eva can't understand him very well. She hears the buzzing of voices. The guests have arrived.

Lisa! Lisa is still sitting on the toilet. She must return to bed immediately.

Eva sneaks into the hall and opens the bathroom door. There is Lisa. Her pajama bottom is lying on the floor.

"Come," Eva says softly. "Hurry up."

"I'll sit here until they're gone," Lisa whispers.

"You don't have to. We'll be very quiet. Leave your pants on the floor."

They tiptoe back to bed and lie close to each other once again. "Let's go to sleep," says Eva.

Eva is awakened by the sound of the radio. The voices she hears are speaking in German, for Aunt Martha and Uncle Eduard often listen to the German station. Eva herself has even heard Hitler speak. He shouted so loudly that she had to put her fingers in her ears to block out that horrible voice. But this is not the radio! These are real people. They are singing a birthday song for Aunt Martha. What song could that be?

Carefully she slides out of bed and lies down with her ear to the floor. The voices downstairs become louder:

"Teun . . . Mies . . . Mies . . . Does, and Gijs—"

This is not a birthday song. They are singing the words from a reading slate! Eva begins to laugh. How strange grown-ups can be sometimes, she thinks.

Suddenly they begin to sing another song. Eva is startled. She doesn't think she has heard it correctly.

"Auf der Heide steht ein kleines Blümelein . . ." shout the voices. They are singing the same song that she heard four years ago, when the German soldiers marched into Rotterdam.

"Schön ist die Jugendzeit . . . schön ist die Jugendzeit . . ."

Eva knows for sure that the people downstairs will celebrate Aunt Martha's birthday first, then come upstairs to arrest her and her sleeping sister.

Listen. They are coming already! Eva can hear the metal on their boots tapping against the wooden steps.

She jumps back into bed. They will find her now. In a couple of seconds a Nazi will pull away the covers and shout, "Get dressed! I'm taking you to Westerbork. Hurry up!"

They *must* climb out of the window and get away from here. But Lisa doesn't even have her pajama bottom on.

"Mama, help!" Eva cries, deep under the covers. "Help!"

SCHOKOLADE

"LOOK WHAT I HAVE HERE," SAYS AUNT MARTHA, and she holds a chocolate bar above her head. "This chocolate is very unusual."

Lisa reaches for the candy. Aunt Martha places two white chunks in her hand.

Lisa puts one piece in her mouth. "Mmm, delicious!" she exclaims. "I'll save the other piece for this evening."

"And you, Marie-Louise?" Aunt Martha crumples the foil wrapper into a silver ball. She takes the colored paper that covered the foil and throws it on the table. "Don't you want any, Marie-Louise? What's the matter with you? It's been a long time since you've eaten chocolate. Why don't you want it?" She offers a piece to Eva. "Here, this is for you."

"No."

"Why not?"

"I'm not telling."

"But I want to know."

"I don't want any Nazi chocolate."

"What did you say? How did you—" Aunt Martha begins to cough. The piece of chocolate that she just put in her mouth falls to the floor. "It went down the wrong way . . . I nearly choked. Wait a minute . . . now tell me," she pants.

"I don't want any Nazi chocolate," Eva repeats.

"Why do you call it that?" Aunt Martha has recovered from her choking spell. She takes a red handkerchief from her stocking and blows her nose.

"It says *'Weisse Schokolade'* on the wrapper," Eva replies, and walks to the table. She picks up the crumpled outer wrapper, unfolds it, and smooths it with her hand. "See? It's in German. It's exactly the same kind of chocolate that a German soldier wanted to give to us at the beginning of the war. And you smoke German cigarettes," she adds accusingly.

Aunt Martha sits on the bed. "Don't ask me

about that," she whispers. "Please don't. I can't explain anything now. Really, it's too dangerous. I'll tell you later, when the war is over."

Lisa picks up her piece of chocolate. "Take this," she says. "I don't want it anymore."

Aunt Martha picks up the wrapper from the table and places Lisa's candy on the book that Eva is reading. "Do you think you'll change your mind?" she asks.

"No." Lisa presses her lips together. "I don't want any Nazi chocolate either."

"I'm going downstairs," says Aunt Martha. "The milkman could come at any moment. But there is one thing you must know: the situation is very different from what you think."

"*We* don't think anything," says Eva.

Aunt Martha closes the door behind her. They hear her walking down the stairs. A bit later comes the distant sound of pans clattering in the kitchen.

Eva sits on the table and swings her legs back and forth. "I know how Aunt Martha got that chocolate," she remarks. "Didn't you hear anything last night?"

"Last night? No." Lisa shrugs. "What should I have heard?"

"Germans. They were downstairs."

"Downstairs? In the living room?"

"Yes. They were singing German songs, and *you* with your bare bottom slept through it."

"You're crazy." Lisa taps her finger on her forehead. "You're absolutely crazy."

"You'll have to hear it for yourself if you don't believe me." Eva is practically shouting. "I'll wake you up if they come again."

They do come! Once again Aunt Martha says that they must eat early because she and Uncle Eduard will be having company. Once again she says that they must be dead still.

"I'll stay awake," Lisa decides. "I want to hear who it is."

They don't have to wait very long. At about eight o'clock the hallway becomes filled with guests once again. They are loud at first, but the noise gradually diminishes.

"They're in the living room now," Lisa whispers. "But there aren't any Nazis. You liar; you were just trying to scare me."

"Then what about that chocolate and those cigarettes?" Eva whispers back.

They hear the buzzing of voices and the

ringing of the kitchen timer. Could Aunt Martha be cooking?

It has grown quiet downstairs. The visitors must be eating now. Perhaps they are having sauerkraut and sausage.

"I crave sauerkraut. Do you?" Eva whispers.

Lisa doesn't answer, for all at once they hear Hitler's voice. He is shouting very loudly. They put their hands over their ears, but it doesn't help; his ranting penetrates to the upstairs.

"I want to leave," Lisa cries. "I hear Germans downstairs. When they finish eating their sauerkraut, they'll come upstairs and get us. I don't want to be arrested!"

"Shh. Don't move and don't talk." Eva slides her arm under Lisa's left shoulder. "Calm down."

"Here they come!" Lisa dives under the covers and crawls to the foot of the bed.

Eva lies quietly and presses her hands against her stomach. Why don't they close the door to the living room? She doesn't want to hear those German voices.

"Close the windows, please." Uncle Eduard's voice.

"Hitler kaput!" shouts a voice.

"Saukerl!" shouts another.

"That's a German," says Lisa quietly. "They have a lot of nerve. In a little while they'll take Aunt Martha and Uncle Eduard with them, and then we'll have to stay here all by ourselves."

"The living room door is open," Eva whispers. "I can hear everything. And Hitler keeps right on shouting."

"Zum Wohl!" a man's voice calls out. *"Zum Wohl*, Gröger, Schmidt . . . Bauer!"

The sound of footsteps. The Germans are in the hall now. The time has come; they're going to be caught! They crawl back under the covers as fast as they can.

They hear footsteps by their bed.

"Come on out." Uncle Eduard's voice. "I want to explain something to you."

Lisa appears first, then Eva.

"I have the feeling that you're badly frightened by the visitors downstairs."

The girls nod.

"Do you think that you can keep a huge, enormous secret?"

They nod again. "We promise," says Lisa, speaking just as solemnly as she did when she made the pledge to Eva, Davy, and Doortje.

"Get out of bed, Marie-Louise. You can climb

right back in again. I have something important to say, and I want to sit in between you two while I tell it."

Eva does as she is told. They are sitting straight up, with their backs leaning against the pillows. Uncle Eduard puts an arm around each girl.

"Here is the secret," he whispers. "These Germans are all against Hitler."

"How do you know that?" whispers Eva.

"Alas, I can't tell you anything more. But I wanted to share this information with you so that you won't be scared when they come back again."

"I *am* scared," says Lisa. "I'm scared to death. But I don't hear them anymore."

"That's right. I told them that they would have to be a little quieter. They've had a bit too much to drink. Did you hear what they were saying?"

"I did," Eva answers. "*Hitler kaput!* and *Saukerl*. Is that bad?"

Uncle Eduard laughs. "Yes," he says. "*Saukerl* means 'rotten fellow.'" He stops laughing and becomes very serious all of a sudden.

"There is one more thing you must know."

He is speaking so softly that the girls can barely understand him. "If the Sicherheitsdienst finds out that these Germans can't stand Hitler, they'll be arrested and possibly sent to a camp or—"

"Shot," says Lisa. "It would serve them right."

"You wouldn't be talking like that if you knew the whole story," says Uncle Eduard. "When the war is over, we'll tell you everything."

"Do they know that we're here?" asks Eva.

"I believe that Aunt Martha has told them about you."

"She shouldn't have said anything." Lisa moves to the foot of the bed. "She *shouldn't* have. They're going to betray us."

"These are not bad Germans, Lisa. Please believe me."

"Good Germans don't exist," Lisa replies with a snarl.

Private Gröger

"Quick, get dressed." Uncle Eduard is standing in the room all of a sudden. "There's something amiss."

"Has someone been caught?" Eva asks.

"Yes, and I want to tell you about it right now. It concerns a German who has been a frequent visitor here."

"A German from the group that brought the chocolate and the Ky-Kyriazi cigarettes?" Eva can barely pronounce the word.

"Right. The Germans you were so afraid of."

"We're always afraid of Germans," says Lisa.

"Well, one of the German soldiers—Gröger by name—joined our resistance group. All the Dutch members felt safe because of his German uniform. But Gröger has now been caught. He helped blow up a town hall somewhere in Holland, together with eleven other people. They all were betrayed, and all twelve were arrested."

"That German is going to betray *us*," says Lisa.

"I don't think he will. Still, I want to bring you somewhere else because it will be safer that way. Martha has already fled to another address. Come, get your coats on, take your underwear, and let's go."

Uncle Eduard walks to the wardrobe. "Here are your coats. Hurry."

"Where are we going?" Eva must bite her lip to keep from crying.

"I can't tell you, but you'll know soon," he answers. "If we're stopped, you'll give them your false name. Who are you? Quick, we don't have much time."

"I'm Marie-Louise Dutour."

"Why are you here?"

"I fled after the bombing of Rotterdam."

"Where are your parents?"

"Dead."

"That could very well be true," says Lisa. "And I'm Marie-Jeanne Dutour."

"Come, let's go. And when you're outside, don't run. Walk slowly, like ordinary children." Uncle Eduard is almost down the stairs. "Come down the steps. Don't be afraid. I'll tell you a joke on the way."

The sun is shining much brighter than it used to. The streets are more crowded than they used to be, and everyone is looking at them.

Lisa puts her hand over her eyes. "It's so light," she whispers. "I don't like being outside at all."

"Keep walking and talk in an ordinary voice," Uncle Eduard says quietly.

He looks at Eva. "How was school, Marie-Louise?"

The girls are startled, for he is speaking very loudly now.

"Fine."

"Did you do well on your dictation?"

Eva nods.

They walk the rest of the way in silence. They pass the municipal hospital, some shops, and a police station. At last they stop in front of a large house. Uncle Eduard knocks three times on a window. Their hearts skip a beat as the door opens.

"Come in." A stout woman is standing in the doorway. "You must go, Eduard," she says. "The sooner, the better."

Uncle Eduard nods. "Good-bye, children. I'll give Henny your new address." He pats them on the head. "Nice little brunettes, aren't they?" he says to the woman.

She nods and shuts the door. Then she turns to Eva and Lisa.

"I'm Big Mie," she says with a smile. "That's what everyone calls me. Come on in."

She leads the girls into a large room. "This is the living room," she says. "Don't be afraid." She points to the head of a deer that is hanging above the heater.

"I can see that you're frightened, little maid," she says to Lisa. "But it's stone dead, and that one is too." She points to the head of a pig. "That's a wild boar. When the neighborhood children come here to eat pancakes, they like to stand on a chair and tickle it under its chin."

Big Mie points to another wall. "The guns over there belonged to my father," she explains. "He brought down many a beast with those things."

"How creepy!" says Lisa, and she shudders. "Dead animals make me sick to my stomach.

Where is our hiding place?"

"Here in this room. You may stay in the living room. It's only when visitors come that you'll have to go to your hiding place. And when there are too many Germans on the street, when there's a roundup."

"You mean, we can just stay here in the living room?" Eva looks at Big Mie in surprise. "But we're . . . we're—"

"I know. You are Jewish children, but children can't be put away the whole day, not even Jewish children. That's how I feel about it at least."

"Do you think that we could eat pancakes with the neighborhood children?" Lisa asks.

Big Mie pulls Lisa onto her lap. "In a little while, when we're free," she replies. "Then we'll invite all the children in the village to come over and eat pancakes with you. But we can't do it now, unfortunately. When the children are here, you will have to leave the room. But I'll save the biggest, fattest pancakes for you. And when my husband gets home, he'll show you your actual hiding place."

"Of course we'll have to be dead still in that hiding place," says Eva. "And we can't cough. Is the hiding place in a cabinet?"

"You're thinking about Davy and Doortje, aren't you?" Lisa whispers.

Eva nods. "And about Ali too," she whispers back.

Big Mie shakes her head. Her cheeks shake as well. "No, it's not in a cabinet," she answers. "I'll get you something to drink now, and I'll make some sandwiches for later. You must be hungry and thirsty."

"Do you think she's nice?" whispers Lisa when Big Mie has left the room.

"I don't know. Maybe."

"I think she's nice. And we get big fat pancakes to eat, and maybe we won't have to leave, and—"

Lisa stops talking all of a sudden. She looks wide-eyed at her sister. "Papa and Mama—how will they know that we're here? What if Uncle Eduard is arrested on his way home? Then he won't be able to tell Henny where we are. *She* thinks we're still at Aunt Martha's house."

Eva is startled. What can she say to Lisa to comfort her?

"She'll . . . she'll . . . go . . . to . . ." Eva stammers. She can't think of anything to say. "I think Big Mie is very nice," she continues. "And

Papa and Mama will find us. Fathers and mothers can smell where their children are. Just like the giant in the story of Jack and the Beanstalk, who called, 'I smell human flesh.' Our parents will call, 'I smell Lisa flesh . . . I smell Eva flesh.'"

Lisa begins to laugh. Soon she is laughing so hard that she can barely stop.

"Shh. You mustn't do that, Lisa. Be quiet, stupid. We're brand-new here."

"I've brought you some punch to drink," says Big Mie, and she enters the room with a large, round serving tray. It seems as though she is carrying it not only with her hands but with her stomach as well. "Drink up!" she says. "And here comes Rinus!"

They hear some peculiar sounds in the hall. "Rinus is taking off his wooden shoes," Big Mie explains. "It's been a long time since we've lived in the country, but he won't give up his wooden shoes."

The door swings open. "Welcome, girls," the man says in a deep voice. "I'm Skinny Rinus, Big Mie's husband." He pulls Eva's pigtail. "And who are you?"

"I'm Marie-Louise Dutour," she whispers.

"Is that your real name?" he asks, putting his

hand on Eva's shoulder. "I know everything. Henny told me about you a long time ago. You can trust me. Now say your real name very quietly."

"I'm . . . I'm Eva Zilverstijn. Aunt Martha is in hiding now too. A soldier named Gröger was caught, and Ali was caught a long time ago."

"Hello, Eva Zilverstijn," Skinny Rinus whispers in her ear. "Don't tell me so much, my girl."

"And I'm Lisa Zilverstijn!" She walks up to Rinus and extends her hand.

"Hello, Lisa Zilverstijn," he says in her ear.

"Hello, Mr. Skinny Rinus," she answers. "Is that your real name?"

Skinny Rinus puts his other hand on Lisa's shoulder. "I have an order for both of you," he says. "Every day for five minutes, you must say your real names out loud. Not those silly French names, but your own true names. In that way you'll never forget who you are."

"Thank you, sir," says Eva.

"Thank you, Mr. Skinny Rinus," says Lisa. "Will you let us stay here?"

"You may stay here, even if it's for the rest of your lives," he answers with a smile.

MOVIE

NOW THAT EVA AND LISA ARE LIVING WITH Skinny Rinus and Big Mie, it's not bad at all to have scabies. Each evening they stand side by side, stark naked, and wait to be rubbed with Scabinol. Every inch of their bodies must be covered with the ointment, which stinks like sulfur.

"Arms up!" Big Mie calls, and they feel as though they are back in gym class. "Arms down! Turn around!" When she is finished, she gives each of them a smack on the bottom and it doesn't even hurt. Big Mie's hands are very gentle, much gentler than Aunt Martha's. She laughed when Lisa remarked about the difference.

"It's because I have so much love in my hands," she said. "Look, these rolls of fat are full of love. That's why my hands are so chubby."

Every evening they have clean nightgowns to wear, and every evening they lie between clean sheets.

"In this way your scabies will soon be gone," Big Mie explains. "That's what Nurse Henny taught me. 'Cleanliness is the enemy of scabies,' she said. You've already had enough misery in your lives. You don't need this itching too."

"Do you want to get better soon?" asks Lisa when they lie in bed at night. "Do *you* want to get rid of your scabies?"

"Of course. I'm sick to death of our smell. And I think that the warmer it is outside, the more we stink." Eva turns over. She doesn't feel like talking anymore.

"No, wait." Lisa pokes her in the back. "I want to keep my scabies, and you know the reason why."

"Shut up. Don't be such an idiot."

"But I want to talk."

"Why?"

"I don't want to go away. They're so nice here. And on Wednesdays we get big fat pancakes to eat."

Eva sits up. "We don't have to leave," she says. "Skinny Rinus told us that we could stay here for the rest of our lives, didn't he?"

"For the rest of our lives? But I don't want that at all."

"No, of course not. I don't either. We'll stay here until the Nazis are gone, and then we'll go home."

"To what home?" Lisa pulls Eva's hair. "Well? What home?"

"I don't know. We'll see. Now go to sleep." Eva turns back over again.

"Stupid girl," Lisa mutters. "The smell and the heat are choking me too."

It is not as warm as it was yesterday. The yellow sunflowers on the curtains are not as bright as they were the day before. It seems as though the storm and the rain last night washed all the colors away. Eva sees a patch of gray light through a crack in the curtains. Lisa is still sleeping. One of her pigtails is lying on her neck, just like a black snake that moves a bit when she breathes.

The church clock chimes. It is five o'clock.

Eva looks at the brown ceiling. What a shame

it is that there are only heavy beams instead of angels upon it. Little Emanuel at Aunt Martha's house will probably miss her.

"Eva!"

She looks at Lisa. Her braid moves up and down as she breathes.

"Eva! Psst . . . here, between the second and third beams. Here I am!"

Eva looks up. Over there, hovering beneath the ceiling, is Davy. He extends his arms.

"Hello, Eva."

"Hello, Davy. How are you?"

"Fine. Don't speak too loudly, or you'll be caught."

"*You* were caught, weren't you?"

"Yes."

"Don't talk about that. I already know."

"You mustn't get better, Eva. If you have scabies, the Nazis will be afraid of you."

"Wait, Davy. Would you like to have scabies too? Here's my nightgown. I'll throw it to you. Scabies is contagious," says Eva, and she pulls her nightgown over her head.

"Ow, what are you doing?" Lisa rubs her eyes. "You're punching me. Bah, the sun is coming out again. It'll be hot today."

"There . . . up above . . . Davy!"

Lisa looks wide eyed at the ceiling.

"There, between the second and third beams," says Eva, and she points. "Look!"

"I don't see anything," says Lisa. "Only a puddle of water!"

Eva sees it too. There is water on the ceiling, and it's moving. "How pretty," she whispers. "But I don't see Davy anymore."

"I don't see him either," Lisa whispers back, "but I see water moving on the ceiling, and the ceiling isn't wet."

"Do you know what we'll do?" Eva slips off her pillowcase. "We'll make a movie screen. There are some thumbtacks in the hall closet. If we attach the pillowcase to the ceiling, it will be just like watching a real movie."

She tiptoes to the hall. The closet door creaks as she opens it. On a shelf is the little box of copper thumbtacks. She wants to hide it in the pocket of her nightgown, but suddenly she notices that she isn't wearing anything. She is completely naked! Imagine if Rinus were to see her like this. She would die of shame.

Eva returns to the bedroom and puts her nightgown back on. Lisa is still watching the ceiling. "That water is so pretty," she says with a sigh. "And we'll have a movie screen too."

"You'll have to help me," Eva whispers. "We'll take the pillowcase off the ceiling at eight o'clock, because when Big Mie comes upstairs she might get angry if she sees it. We'll put it back up tomorrow, if the water is still there. Come, I'll stand on a chair, and you'll climb up on my shoulders. Together we'll be tall enough to reach the ceiling."

She stands on a brown wooden chair.

"We're a tower!" Lisa exclaims. "It's just like being in a circus. Attention, ladies and gentlemen. Come and see the living tower of the Ezi–Lizi Circus!" She extends her leg. "Your attention, please!"

"Shut up!" Eva snaps. "I'll let you fall if you keep being so silly. Come on, put in those tacks!"

Lisa must push hard on the thumbtacks. When she has six of them in place, they have a wonderfully tight movie screen. They climb back into bed, and with wide eyes they watch their film of colors and water. Red, orange, yellow, green . . .

"It's so beautiful, just like in a fairy tale," Lisa whispers.

"What are you girls doing?"

They did not hear Big Mie enter the room.

"Tell me, what are you doing?" She looks from the bed to the ceiling. "What's that?"

"A movie screen," Eva whispers.

"A movie screen?" says Big Mie, and she puts her hands on her hips. "Move over. I'm going to lie down next to you because I want to see that movie too."

The bed makes a loud, creaking sound as she climbs in. "The bed doesn't want me, but I *must* see your movie," she says, laughing.

All three watch the ceiling.

"My goodness, you're right!" Big Mie exclaims. "I didn't believe you. How can this be? It looks just like water glittering in the sunlight."

"We don't know," Lisa says, and giggles. "And Eva has seen Davy. *He* wants to get scabies too."

Big Mie sits on the edge of the bed. "Don't talk for a moment," she says. "I've got to think about this."

She remains motionless. "Right," she says at last. "It might be that." She walks to the window and opens the curtains a bit more.

"Look at your screen now," she says.

"The water is on the screen and is next to the screen too!" calls Lisa.

"And now?" Big Mie closes the curtains all the way.

"The movie has disappeared," says Eva. "How can that be?"

"Look again." Big Mie opens the curtains a little.

"It's back!" Lisa says, and climbs out of bed.

"Look carefully between the curtains," Big Mie says with a smile. "What do you see?"

"A deep puddle of water on the roof of the scullery," Eva replies.

"That's right. And what you see on the ceiling is the reflection of the puddle."

"May we look again?" Eva asks.

"Of course you may. But if the sun shines as much as it did yesterday, the puddle will evaporate, and your movie will disappear too."

"How awful," Lisa says with a sigh. "I want to watch the movie all day long."

"I can understand that," says Big Mie. "But I have an idea. A friend of mine has a movie projector and lots of cartoons. I'll ask her if we may borrow everything. You'll be able to see real movies then. I'll just tell her that Rinus and I want to go back to our childhoods, when times were peaceful. Aartje has movies of Popeye and

Donald Duck and Betty Boop."

"Betty Poop?" Lisa is laughing so hard that she has fallen on the bed. "Did you hear that, Eva? Betty Poop?"

"Not so loud, Marie-Jeanne." Big Mie admonishes her. "Shh! Her name is Betty Boop. B-O-O-P."

"I don't want to see the water anymore," says Eva. "But I'll keep watching the ceiling. Maybe Davy will come back."

Big Mie strokes her head. "You are a dear, Marie-Louise," she says.

"You must say, 'Eva, what a dear you are,'" says Lisa. "We're supposed to be called Eva and Lisa Zilverstijn for five minutes every day, aren't we? Skinny Rinus said so himself."

"That's right," says Big Mie, and she laughs. "Eva and Lisa Zilverstijn, you are both such dears."

PANCAKES

"WELL, THAT'S THAT." SKINNY RINUS PUTS TWO plates on the table. "You girls must eat without us. We're too busy. The pancake eaters will be here in half an hour. You'll have potatoes, red cabbage, and a cutlet. Doesn't that sound good?"

"Hmm," grumbles Lisa.

"It's a shame that you can't be downstairs this afternoon," says Rinus with a sigh. "But we can't do anything about it. We never know who will be coming. There's a sign hanging on our fence that says all the children in the neighborhood are welcome. Sometimes the neighborhood children bring guests with them—cousins, classmates, children we don't know. We've been serving pancakes for so many years that we don't dare stop now that you're here. Everyone would be suspicious, and we don't want that, do we?"

"Of course not," replies Eva.

"But I do have an idea."

"What?" Lisa asks. "May we go downstairs anyway?"

"Clean your plate first; then we'll see. You don't know what you're in for." Rinus walks to the hall. "Remember, eat your cutlet down to the bone," he calls.

"What kind of surprise does Skinny Rinus have for us?" asks Lisa. "What do you think, Eva?"

"I don't know. Maybe he'll take some black shoe polish and rub it all over us. Then those children wouldn't be able to see who we are."

"Or maybe we'll wear costumes," says Lisa. "A cat costume or a clown costume, with a mask for our eyes."

Eva rests her chin in one hand and with her other hand mashes her red cabbage and potatoes together. "We'll be allowed . . . we'll be allowed to stay downstairs, and Big Mie will tell the children that we're part of the family. Her dead sister's children or something like that."

"I can hardly keep it straight anymore," Lisa says. "I'm a little bit of everything. I'm Marie-Jeanne Dutour. I'm a Huguenot and a refugee from Rotterdam. I'm an orphan, and I'm Big Mie's niece. It's enough to drive me crazy."

"You're already crazy," Eva says to tease her.

Lisa sets her fork in her meat. "I don't want any more," she says. "Otherwise I won't have room for the pancakes when all those awful children are gone. What do I hear, Eva?" She looks at the ceiling. A strange noise is coming from above; it sounds like a dentist's drill, but it's much louder.

"I think that Skinny Rinus is taking our bedroom apart," whispers Eva. "What a racket!"

"If we no longer have our bedroom to hide in, we'll *have* to stay down here," says Lisa, and she laughs. "Listen. The noise has stopped. He's finished."

"Well, here I am. Did you enjoy your meal, children? Let's go upstairs now and see the surprise." Skinny Rinus sets a large drill down on the floor. "Goodness, that was heavy. I borrowed it from my neighbor Mr. Brandsen. That man is drowning in tools, he has so many of them."

"May we see what our surprise looks like?" asks Eva.

"What it looks like?" Skinny Rinus glances at her and points to the drill. "This is part of the surprise. Let's go up now."

He gives Eva a little push. "Come on upstairs, girls. You won't believe your eyes. Do you have any idea what the surprise might be?"

Eva shrugs and looks at Lisa.

Lisa shakes her head. "I don't know either."

Skinny Rinus takes his handkerchief and wipes the sweat from his forehead. "Whew, what a job! But I was happy to do it for you."

"Did you take our room apart?" asks Eva.

"Something like that," he answers. "Let's go upstairs. Be careful!"

Eva leads the way. She stumbles into the bedroom. "Ow!" she shouts. "What's happened here?"

"I pulled up a piece of the linoleum for you," Skinny Rinus says, smiling. "You tripped over the mess. Come here." He points to the wooden floor. "Here in this corner, behind your bed. There it is."

"I don't see anything," says Lisa.

"Lie down on the floor here." He points to a spot where a small cabinet stood. "Stoop down by this board. What do you see?"

"A little hole," Lisa replies.

"Right. Now lie down and look through

that hole. What do you see?"

"I see Big Mie!" Lisa shouts. "There, down-tairs. We can see everything downstairs."

"My turn!" Eva tries to push her sister away. "Please, Lisa. May I look now?"

"She's set the table and . . . and . . . "

"Well, what do you say?" Skinny Rinus looks from Lisa to Eva. "Say something. In this way you'll feel a little bit like you're downstairs too."

Lisa stands and walks up to Skinny Rinus. "You are the nicest foster father I've ever had," she declares.

"Take turns looking, and remember to be quiet, all right?" he says. "I'm going to help Big Mie now. I'll pick up the linoleum this evening."

He blows his nose and wipes his eyes. "I fall apart when I get a compliment like that. But I'll be darned if it isn't true."

"What do you see, Eva?"

"I see a whole lot of children and a big stack of pancakes and clean white plates that have a blue rim," she whispers. "Big Mie is walking around the table. She is putting a pancake on the plate of a girl . . . no, it's a boy. It's difficult to tell. I can see only the tops of their heads and their shoulders. I can't tell if they're wearing slacks or dresses because they're hidden under the table."

"My turn," Lisa whispers. "Move away."

"In a minute. They're picking up their forks now. I see a big fat boy. He's eating a rolled-up pancake. Ugh, the syrup is dripping down his hands. It's your turn now."

"Where is that boy, that big fat one?" Lisa whispers.

"Near the window. See him?"

"Yes. And he's not eating, he's guzzling. I can hear him smacking his lips. All the children have blond hair."

"Are they drinking anything?"

"Yes. Punch, I think. Do you want another turn? I've seen enough." Lisa stands and brushes the dust from her dress. "It *is* fun to look, but it's not entirely fun."

Eva stretches out on the floor again. "I don't feel like watching them anymore either. I only feel like spitting on their heads. Shall I do it?"

"Are you crazy?" says Lisa, and tries to pull her sister up. "Soon they'll notice that we're here and then—"

"I'm not crazy. Do you think that I want to be caught?" Eva rolls over on her back. She puts her hands behind her head and closes her eyes, as though she is sunbathing. "Sometimes I do want to be caught," she says quietly. "If we were caught, we would no longer have to be afraid of being caught. Do you feel that way too?"

Lisa nods. "Sometimes. Then I want to stand in front of a window and scream. But all at once I become so afraid that I really *will* scream that I get a stomachache."

Eva nods. "I've felt that way too," she says. "You should listen to what's going on downstairs. It's your turn to look."

Lisa lies down again. "I see two lines of children. The first ones in each line are putting their hands together. Oh, no, they're starting to sing too."

"White swan, black swan,
  Who will sail with us to England?
  England has locked its door,
  The key lies buried near the shore,
  The key is lost, the key is lost.
  Isn't there anyone then
  Who can bring the key back home again?
  Let them through, let them through,
  We'll catch . . . you!"

Lisa stands up and beats a cloud of dust from her dress once again. "Do you want to take a look, Eva?"

"No, I don't. Come, let's take a walk. We'll go into a big forest. Do you see the oak and the birch trees? You can smell the earth because it has just rained. We can hear a bird knocking on a tree. It's a woodpecker, and it's calling, 'Let me come in!'"

"'It's cold and bleak and my coat is so thin,'" Lisa sings. "'Let me come in, let me come in . . .'"

"Who wants another pancake?" they hear someone shout.

"*I* do," whispers Eva.

"I do too!" whispers Lisa.

ANTIQUE GUNS

HENNY COMES TO VISIT THEM AT SEVEN O'CLOCK every Friday evening. They look forward to her visits, not only because she is nice but because she brings so many things for them: library books, games, and occasionally a small cake. When they first arrived and were still suffering from scabies, she even gave them a piece of chocolate. She hasn't brought them any since, however, even though they have a craving for it.

"Remember the *Weisse Schokolade*, Eva?" Lisa asks every now and then. She doesn't often bring up the subject, though, because thinking about Private Gröger makes them feel so sad. Not long ago Henny told them that Karl Gröger was shot in July, together with his eleven Dutch friends.

"And he was only twenty-five," Henny said.

"I loved him very much." She began to weep then, and Eva and Lisa wept too.

What a shame that it is only Thursday. The girls must wait more than twenty-four hours before they see Henny.

There is a visitor downstairs. They can hear his voice mingling with the voices of Big Mie and Skinny Rinus.

"Do you want to see what he looks like?" asks Lisa.

"*You* look. I want to finish my book. Henny will be coming with more books tomorrow," Eva replies.

Lisa carefully moves the cabinet to the side, then lies down on the floor.

"Oh, no! It can't be a policeman, can it? Come here, Eva." She slides over a bit. "Hurry!"

Eva lies down next to her. "It *is* a policeman. I can see his cap. Now be quiet!"

"You could be punished," they hear. "You should have turned them in."

"We—we should have been turned in," Lisa stammers.

"Shut up," Eva snaps. "I want to listen. That policeman is standing up now. He's walking to the living room door."

"You must take my warning very seriously." The voice is in the hall now. "They won't find out about it today, but they'll know by tomorrow or the day after. . . . Adieu."

"Thank you, van Beurden." Skinny Rinus's voice. The front door closes.

Eva kneels with her hands over her eyes.

"What's happened?" Lisa is nearly in tears.

"I don't know, but it must be something very bad. I'm sure of it." Eva can't sit still; she is trembling all over and is ice cold all of a sudden.

"Come here," Lisa whispers. "Give me your hands. I'll warm them up." She kneels and begins to rub Eva's fingers, but it's no use. Eva is shaking so badly that Lisa begins to shake as well.

They can hear Big Mie talking down below.

"Skinny Rinus isn't saying anything," whispers Lisa.

"Then she must be on the telephone," Eva replies.

"Sweethearts, what is the matter? You look like two little drowned birds. Come, stand up." Big Mie reaches out to the girls. "Give me your hands. I'll help you up."

"We have to be turned in," Lisa sobs. "We heard it ourselves. There was a policeman downstairs."

"That's true, but dry your eyes. He's a very good policeman." Big Mie pulls them toward the bed. "Come, I'll tell you about him. He pretends to be friendly to the Germans, but when he hears about an upcoming roundup or a shooting, he warns people about it right away. This is a big secret, you understand."

They nod. "So we'll have to leave," says Eva.

"Perhaps, but it doesn't have anything to do with you. Apparently one of the boys who came to eat pancakes yesterday saw the guns belonging to my great-great-grandfather. The boy told his father about them, and the father reported to the Germans that Skinny Rinus and Big Mie are in possession of weapons that should have been turned in before September 20, 1940."

"What a rotten boy," exclaims Lisa. "What a dirty, rotten traitor."

"Yes, and his father too." Big Mie shakes her head. "I'm sure that fellow will receive money for his betrayal. We're bought and betrayed nowadays. I've called Henny to ask her what to do. She'll be coming soon."

"I'll go pack my bag," says Eva, and she sighs. "We'll have to leave."

"It's probably better that way," says Big Mie. "You never know what those horrible Nazis are going to do. But don't think that it's going to be so easy to find another address for you."

She looks at Eva and Lisa as though she is seeing them for the very first time. "My goodness, it's going to be hard to find you a new home. That dark hair of yours is lovely, but it makes the situation difficult and dangerous indeed."

"Listen carefully," says Henny. "When it's dark, I'll take you to a place far away from here. You'll never know how I came upon this new address."

"Naturally from the underground," says Eva.

"Wrong."

"From . . . from . . . I don't know. I give up."

"From your parents."

"From Papa and Mama?"

"Right. I phoned someone who knows your parents well and said I had two pairs of children's shoes left but wasn't sure of the size."

"That's just what Ali said when we had to go to Uncle Eduard and Aunt Martha without Papa and Mama," says Lisa quietly. "Did you say your name backward too? And where are we going?"

"Yes, I said I was Yne. That's almost my name. And I can't tell you where we're going. You learned long ago that it's dangerous to know too much."

"Are we leaving now?" asks Eva, putting a pair of blue socks in her bag.

"In a little while," says Henny. "I have something for you. It's from your parents. Close your eyes and put your hands out."

They do as they're told, standing motionless as they wait to receive their surprise.

"Look!" Henny calls.

"Our clown!" Eva screams. "Look, Lisa, we have our clown back!" She presses the painting to her face. "Here, a kiss on your red hair."

"That clown will protect you on the long trip we'll be making together," says Henny. Her voice suddenly sounds very strange.

"What about Papa and Mama?" asks Eva. "Maybe Mama still has a little bit of jaundice."

"Believe me, you need that little clown more than they do at the moment because we have some walking to do." Henny takes the bag from Eva's hand. "Put your mascot in here," she says.

"Do we have to walk? Where are we going? Won't it be dangerous?" asks Lisa, pulling on Henny's coat.

Lisa turns to Big Mie. "Won't it be dangerous, Big Mie?"

Big Mie wraps her arms around Lisa and holds her close. "Staying here would be even more dangerous," she says, trying to comfort her. "I'm so sorry about those guns. We didn't know we were supposed to turn in those antique weapons. I'm sure the Nazis will be coming to take us away, as punishment."

"Give Big Mie a kiss," Henny whispers in Lisa's ear.

"What about Skinny Rinus?" asks Lisa. "I want to say good-bye to him too."

"Skinny Rinus is gone." Big Mie begins to cry. She takes a handkerchief from her pocket. "He's going into hiding, just like you," she sputters. "He has such an awful time saying good-bye. At least he won't have to do that now."

Henny walks to the stairs. "Come, children, let's go. You know what you're supposed to say if we're stopped, don't you?"

"I'm Marie-Jeanne Dutour. My father and

mother are dead, and I'm from Rotterdam," Lisa drones.

"And how about you?" Henny asks, looking at Eva.

"I'm—I'm—I can't remember."

"Your real name is Eva Zilverstijn, but you must say that you're Marie-Louise Dutour," says Big Mie, trying to help her. "Farewell, children. Farewell, and have a good car trip."

She embraces Eva. "Good-bye for now, sweetheart. I'll see you when the war is over."

"Are we going in a car?" asks Eva. "But we're walking, aren't we?"

"Don't ask so many questions, Marie-Louise," Henny replies sternly. "You'll see for yourself. Now get going. Forward, march!"

BANDAGES

"WE'RE GOING TO STOP HERE FIRST," HENNY whispers.

"At a park?" says Eva.

"Shh. Yes, at a park. Don't ask any more questions. Sit down on this bench."

"How nice it smells outside," Lisa whispers. "So green."

"Don't be afraid." Henny takes something out of her bag. "I'm going to wrap this around your head, Marie-Jeanne," she says quietly. "Come here."

She takes Lisa's braids and pins them on top of her head with a hairpin she has been holding between her lips. Then she begins to wrap a bandage around Lisa's head.

"I'll choke!" Lisa tries to shout.

"You won't choke," says Henny. "I have to do this."

When Lisa's face is barely visible, Henny takes a small brown tube from her bag. She sprinkles some red liquid on the bandage. "Well, you're finished. It's your turn now, Marie-Louise," she says, setting the tube on the bench.

"It looks like Lisa has had a terrible accident," Eva whispers. "How scary. What are we supposed to say if we're stopped?"

"Nothing at all. We won't be stopped, and if we are, I'll do the talking. You won't notice a thing."

"How can that be?" Eva confronts Henny. "Tell me what's going on. All these secrets are driving me crazy."

"Sweetheart, I *can't*. Do you think I enjoy keeping all these secrets from you? But I have to, for your safety and mine. Come, we must hurry." She looks at the watch that is hanging from her white apron. "Quick, it's your turn."

She takes a lump of putty and presses it on Eva's forehead.

"Ow!" Eva puts her hand over her mouth.

Henny holds the little tube and pours some red liquid on a wad of cotton. Then she applies the wad to Eva's forehead.

"Look in my mirror, Marie-Louise. What do you see?"

"I see myself, and I have a big gash on my forehead."

"That's right. You've been seriously injured." Henny is smiling a little, thank goodness. "We'll sit here until an automobile comes by. That auto will give us a special signal. Now let's be quiet."

They remain on the bench, not moving a muscle, with Henny seated in the middle. The only sound is the wind blowing gently through the trees.

"There it is. I think I hear it." Henny jumps up and puts her hand behind her ear. "Yes, that's it."

"I don't hear anything."

"I do. Listen carefully, Marie-Louise. In a few seconds we'll get the signal and—"

They hear a loud noise.

"A siren! Is it an ambulance?" Lisa whispers.

Henny nods. "Come on."

They tiptoe to the park exit.

"There's your transportation," Henny whispers. "Quick, get in."

"Come, girls," they hear someone say.

A man dressed in a white doctor's coat is standing next to the ambulance. "Step in," he says. "Hurry. You too, Henny." He gives her a little push. "Go on. I'll take care of the children."

"No, let me do it," Henny replies, and turns to Eva and Lisa.

"Lie down on that stretcher, Marie-Jeanne." She points to one of the beds. "And your place is there, Marie-Louise." She points to the other bed.

"Where are we going? I have a stomachache." Eva is doubled over in pain.

Henny lays her hand on Eva's head. "Go lie down," she says. "This ambulance is from our hospital, and the driver is one of our nurses. His name is Mr. van—"

"My name isn't important," says the man. "Now, do what we had agreed to do." He reaches into his coat pocket. "Here, take them, Henny," he says, and puts two pink candies in her hand.

"Mmm, candy," exclaims Lisa.

"You'll need to take them with water," says Henny. "They're not candy; they're tranquilizers. One for you"—she puts a small pill in Eva's hand—"and one for you, Marie-Jeanne. Here is some water. Now lie quietly and don't talk. You've just been in an accident, and we're on our way to the emergency room. Understand?"

The girls nod.

Henny sits down between the two stretchers. "Each of you give me your hand," she says. "I'll make sure that you arrive at your new address safe and sound."

"Will there be nice people where we're going?" asks Eva. "Just as nice as Big Mie and Skinny Rinus? And do they have any children?"

"He's a nice man," Henny replies. "A nice man, and he has no children. That is to say, he *does* have children, but they're made of wood and paper. That's all I'm going to say. It's too dangerous to tell you more. Now I'll see how the little one is doing. She's already so quiet."

Henny stands up and waves her hand above Lisa's head. "No reaction," she says loudly.

"What's the matter with Lisa?" Eva asks. She would like to sit up, but she's so dizzy that she can't. "What's the matter with Lisa?" she repeats. Her tongue refuses to form the words she wants to say. She tries to pinch Henny's hand.

"Go ahead. It can't be helped." Henny strokes Eva's cheek and forehead. "Sometimes we must do things to children that we ourselves think are terrible."

Eva tries to grope for Henny's hand, but her arm is so heavy that she can't lift it.

"Where are we going? I don't want to go. I want to stay with Big Mie and Skinny Rinus!" she shouts.

"What did you say?" Henny's ear is right by Eva's mouth. "Tell me again, as loudly as you can. You're speaking so softly that I can't understand you."

Eva tries to look at Henny, but her eyes won't focus.

"Close your eyes," she hears. "Don't fight it. Everything will be all right."

Henny turns to the driver. "It's all under control, Mr. van Velzen," she calls. "They're almost asleep."

Ami Means "Friend"

"Psst, Eva. Here I am. Remember me?"

Eva rubs her eyes. "Where am I?" she asks in a hoarse voice.

"Here, at the foot of your bed. That's where I am."

She looks in the direction of the voice and sees curtains that are unfamiliar to her. Then she sees a painting that *is* familiar; how did their own little clown end up here in this strange room? Whose bed is she in? She sees something move above the foot of the brown wooden bed.

"No!" she shouts. "It *can't* be. You're not Freekie. We left him on the train when we went into hiding. Go away!"

"May I introduce myself? I'm Freekie the Second. My nickname is Freekie Two." The puppet has risen high above the bed.

"Who is moving you?" she asks. "Our Freekie usually spoke in Lisa's voice. But *you* are speaking in a man's voice. Where is Lisa?"

"Lisa is sleeping in my master's bed," Freekie Two answers. "She'll awaken when the sleeping pill has worn off."

Eva sees colors dancing around the doll, resembling the colors of the rainbow: bright red, orange, yellow. A man is floating among the colors.

"Are you all right?" he asks. "Do you remember who I am?"

She tries to look at the man, but she can't. Her eyes keep closing.

"Remember me?"

She attempts to focus upon him again. "Are you . . . are you . . . ?"

"Right. I'm Amici Enfanti: clown, puppeteer, puppet maker, and so on and so forth. From now on you may call me Mr. Ami. Amici Enfanti is too long. *Ami* means 'friend' in French, and that's what I want to be, your friend who protects you from the evil outside world."

He smiles. "Bilthoven, 1939, remember? You spent your vacation next door, in the house belonging to Mr. van der Klyn, the principal of the school. You certainly must remember that I made the doll Freekie and that I painted the clown picture, my self–portrait. I see to my great delight that you've kept the painting. Look, it's hanging over there. Henny told me what happened to your Freekie."

The colors keep dancing around Mr. Ami's head. His voice sounds far away.

"We're still in Enschede, aren't we? Where is Lisa?" asks Eva, and she tries to climb out of bed.

"No, dear. You're in Bilthoven now. Don't get up. Henny brought you here in an ambulance. Your sister is still sleeping."

He pats her on the head. "Sleep," he whispers. "You're safe here. Go back to sleep."

"Freekie is . . . in the train . . . when we . . ."

"Don't talk. Go to sleep. Let the sleeping pill wear off."

"We're now called Marie-Jeanne and Marie-Louise Dutour."

"Not here. You'll be called Eva Zilverstijn in this house. You'll get your real name back again. That Henny certainly must have given you something very strong."

"They were pink. Little pink tablets that

looked like candy and—"

"Sleep . . . go to sleep," Freekie Two whispers. "My master and I will watch over you. There won't be any Germans entering here, or bad Dutchmen either. We'll allow only good people inside."

"But what if the Nazis come?"

"That won't happen. Puppeteers have magic powers. You knew that even before the war began, didn't you?"

A small wooden hand touches her eyelids.

"Shh . . . sleep," whispers Freekie Two.

Yesterday it seemed as though Lisa would sleep forever. Eva spent a long time sitting next to the bed in Mr. Ami's bedroom. Lisa looked so white and lay so still that Eva had to touch her to make sure she was still alive. Fortunately Lisa began to move then. She rubbed her eyes and asked, "What time is it, Big Mie?"

"We're no longer at Big Mie's house," Eva explained. "Remember the ambulance and the pink pills?"

"No." Lisa closed her eyes and went back to sleep. She is wide awake now, thank goodness, but she thinks that she is still at Big Mie's house and only dreaming that she is with Mr. Ami in Bilthoven.

"Pinch your arm or your cheek," Mr. Ami said. "Then you'll know it's not a dream."

"How did we end up here?"

"Henny contacted me at your mother's request. I was so very happy that I could do something for you."

"When do we have to leave?"

"My dear Eva, you may stay here until the war is over."

"That's what Skinny Rinus said too. 'You may stay here, even if it's for the rest of your lives,' he said, but we don't want that, do we, Lisa?"

Mr. Ami picks up Freekie Two. "Of course not," replies the puppet. "When the war is over, I'll go home with you. We don't yet know where that home will be, do we? We don't have anything anymore. No bed, no books, no furnace . . . no . . ."

"As long as you're alive," says Mr. Ami soberly. "That is the most important thing. When I heard about Freekie the First, I felt so bad for you that I made Freekie Two right away. I promised to bring him to Rijswijk after the war. The war isn't even over yet, and he's already with you. Take him, Lisa."

Lisa picks up the puppet. "Do you have a hiding place for us?" she asks.

"No. You'll go to your bedroom when strangers are here. If it becomes very, very necessary, you'll go to the bellefleur cellar."

"You must mean if there's a roundup," says Freekie Two in Lisa's voice. "And what is a belly floor cellar?"

Mr. Ami bursts out laughing. "Not a belly floor cellar but . . . *bellefleur* cellar. A bellefleur is a type of apple. I keep apples in my bellefleur cellar, and grain, potatoes, candles, and much more. You never know if there will be enough food and light."

"And what happens when it's all gone?" asks Freekie Two.

"Then we'll see. Now relax. You're much too young to have so many worries."

"That's right, isn't it?" exclaims Eva, stroking Freekie's little red nose. "You've just been born. You're really just a baby."

"He's no baby," says Mr. Ami, and he smiles. "His head is made from old wood, and his hands too. That's why he says such wise things. As a matter of fact, he's older than any of us."

"It will be difficult to stay here," Lisa comments. "What are we going to do every day? I've read a thousand books already, and I've knit a million socks."

"And we've played I spy eighty thousand times," Eva adds.

"Whoever wants to may help me," Mr. Ami replies. "I'll keep making dolls and doll clothes as long as my wood supply lasts. And I'll put on puppet shows as long as I can. In these times it's even more important to keep the show going."

"I think so too," says Freekie Two. "It's a shame that Eva and Lisa can't be downstairs at the show. Maybe a hole can be drilled in their bedroom floor, just as there was at Skinny Rinus's house."

"A hole in the floor?" Mr. Ami looks at Lisa in surprise. "What do you mean, Freekie Two?"

"I mean . . . I mean . . . that hole allowed them to be downstairs in a way. Lisa told me all about Big Mie and Skinny Rinus," the puppet answers.

"They really *can* be downstairs if they want, Freekie Two. Eva and Lisa Zilverstijn may attend the very first show presented by their friend Amici Enfanti. Excuse me . . . presented by Mr. Ami, their friend."

"No," says Eva. "I don't want to come. A boy betrayed Big Mie and Skinny Rinus by telling the Germans that antique weapons were hanging on their wall. That's why we had to leave. I'll stay upstairs when children are here."

"So will I," says Lisa.

Mr. Ami extends his hand. "Give it here," he tells Lisa. "Give Freekie Two to me."

"Don't be so afraid," says the puppet in a deep voice. "As an authority on children *and* adults, my master has thought of a way for you to be present at the show."

"But we don't dare, Freekie Two," Lisa whispers.

"I know, I know. First comes trust; then your fears will fade away."

"What kind of plan does your master have in mind?"

"I'll tell you later. Here, catch me, Lisa!"

Freekie Two flies through the air. Lisa tries to catch him, but she misses.

"Ouch!" the puppet yells. "My head, my poor head!"

Lisa is so startled by Mr. Ami's outburst that she puts her fingers in her ears. She removes them only when she sees that he has stopped shouting.

"I apologize," says Mr. Ami. "I was very loud, wasn't I? How stupid of me."

"It wasn't stupid at all," says Eva. "I used to be able to shout much, much louder than you."

PIMPINELLIPOLIE

"So, AFTER THREE WEEKS YOU KNOW THAT YOU may mess around as much as you want to in my studio." Mr. Ami looks at Eva and Lisa with satisfaction. "Put on these old shirts of mine. Look, I have clay, brushes, and charcoal. Take what you want. But there's one thing that is off limits: this drawer here." He taps against a shiny brown cabinet. "I can't tell you what I have because it's a secret. But I'll show you what's inside as soon as I think that the end of the war is near."

"I'm going to paint," says Lisa, and she presses a thick gob of red paint from a tube. "This is fun!" she exclaims.

"And you, Eva? What are you going to do?"

"I don't know."

"Look at this lovely clay," says Mr. Ami. "Feel it, pinch it. You can wash your hands when you're finished. I'll get back to work now."

Mr. Ami sits on his stool. He takes a roll of toilet paper and unravels it into a bucket. "There's wallpaper paste in here," he explains. "When the paper has absorbed enough paste, I'll make a doll's head out of it. That head will become as hard as a rock after the paper and paste have dried. Who wants to take over this job for me? Then I can go do something else."

"I will," says Lisa. She pulls a piece of paper from the roll and puts it in the bucket. The paste drips between her fingers. "Ugh, it's nasty," she says, and giggles.

"What about you, Eva?" Mr. Ami stands up. "Don't you want to do anything? Paint, model with clay? Draw with charcoal perhaps?"

"No."

"Then I have something else for you. Wait a minute. I'll be right back."

"He's nice, isn't he?" says Lisa after Mr. Ami has left the room. She wipes her hands on her shirtsleeve. "Come on, we'll take a break. Sit with me, Freekie Two." She picks up the puppet.

"Are you happy, Eva?" Freekie asks.

"Happy? What do you mean, happy?"

"Because Mr. Ami is so nice. Why don't you answer? Don't you think Mr. Ami is nice?"

"Yes, yes, but . . . " Eva is speaking so softly that Lisa must bend across the table to hear her.

"Freekie Two, I'm putting you down," says Lisa. "I think that my sister wants to whisper something in my ear."

The puppet's head makes a bumping sound as it knocks against a wooden table.

"Tell me what's wrong. Whisper it in my ear, Eva."

Eva begins to whisper. Lisa laughs a bit at first, for Eva's breath is tickling her. But as Eva continues to whisper, Lisa's smile gradually fades away.

"Yes," she says when Eva has finished. "Yes, I feel that way too. Shall I get back to work now?"

"All right."

Lisa puts her hand back in the paste once again. "It's so nice to be able to make a mess like this," she comments. "We were never allowed to do this anywhere else, and still—"

"Well, here I am again." Mr. Ami's voice is in the hall. "Quick, open the door, girls. My hands are full."

Lisa rushes to the door. There is Mr. Ami, his face hidden behind a stack of magazines. The peak of his little white hat is barely visible above the pile.

"Eva, these are for you." He plops the magazines down on the table. "Take a pair of scissors and a jar of paste and get going. You can cut up all these antique *Libelle* and *Margriet* magazines and whatever else you come across. I have a sheet of paper for you too. You can make a nice collage by pasting your clippings on it."

It is quiet in the studio now. Lisa stirs the paste, her tongue between her lips. Mr. Ami sits cross-legged on the table, just like a tailor. Now and then he strokes the gold velvet cloth that rests in his lap.

"It's beautiful, master," says Freekie Two in Lisa's voice. "What are you going to make from it? A coat for me perhaps?"

"No, I'm making a king's robe," Mr. Ami whispers. "It will be for King Koerian. His hands and his head are already finished."

Eva sits with a hand under her chin. With her other hand she flips through a *Libelle*. "November 1938," she reads aloud. "Useful tips for making holiday gifts."

"In November 1938 we were still living in Rotterdam, next door to Mrs. Terhegge," says Lisa.

"Mrs. Terhegge has a parrot named Lodewijk," says Mr. Ami with a smile. "Lodewijk always shouted, 'Dirty bastard,' whenever he heard Hitler's name mentioned."

"How do you know that?" asks Lisa.

"I'm a psychic. I know everything," he answers secretively. "I also know that Mrs. Terhegge has a cat named Lena and that Lena had kittens during the bombing of Rotterdam. Mrs. Terhegge gave one of those kittens to you."

"Are you really a psychic?" Lisa asks. "You're right about everything. Do you know that we named our little kitten Mathilde and that she ran away the night before we went into hiding?"

"In August 1939 two sweet girls from Rotterdam were on vacation in Bilthoven at Hoflaan ten for a short time," Mr. Ami whispers. "The puppeteer at Hoflaan twelve made friends with those two little girls. They told him all about Rotterdam. And in June 1940 they sent him a lovely postcard with the picture of a kitten on the front. On the back they wrote, 'This is our kitten, Mathilde, daughter of Lena. Kisses, Eva and Lisa Zilverstijn.'"

"Oh, is that so?"

"Yes, Lisa. Now take a look at your big sister. She doesn't see or hear a thing."

"I don't either," says Lisa. "I'm painting."

It is so quiet in the studio that Lisa's paintbrush can be heard as she applies it to the paper. Now and then comes the sound of paper rustling.

"This is nice. Look on page nine, Lisa. What do you think of that child? Shall I save the page?" asks Eva, and she sets an issue of *Margriet* next to Lisa's painting.

"That girl looks like you," Lisa replies. "She's a miniature Eva, with her glasses and a bow in her hair."

"I can use that picture." Eva tears out the page. Carefully she cuts along the girl's face and along her straight hair with the red bow. She pastes the picture in the center of the white paper.

"Look on page ten," Eva says. "There are all sorts of roses with weird names: Pimpinellipolie . . . Pomifera . . ." She laughs at the complicated names. "Pimpinellipolie, Pomifera," she sings as she cuts out the flowers. She pastes them around little Eva's head, making a frame around the child.

Eva takes the picture of an orange rose called Happiness and clips out only the thorns. She can't stop; it seems as though someone else were moving her hands. She pastes the thorns all around the roses. Suddenly little Eva has a red rose over her heart. She doesn't look as happy as she did a while ago.

"May I look, Eva?" asks Mr. Ami, and he sets the gold velvet on the table. He walks up to Eva and puts his hand on her shoulder.

"Don't," she whispers. "Move your hand. It's making me hot."

He takes the paper in his hands. "Beautiful," he says quietly. "How beautiful. Are you finished?"

"No."

"Then I won't ask any more questions." Mr. Ami sits down on the table again.

Eva picks up a copy of *Libelle*. It looks very old. On the cover is a photograph of a little girl pushing a wicker doll carriage. "'Little mother taking a walk,'" she reads, and bends over the picture. That curl on top of the child's head, those ringlets on the side of her face: Eva has seen that photo before, but where?

She looks at the photo credit on the left side of the picture. "Photograph: Miklos von Vajda," she reads. Miklos von Vajda is . . . She thinks deeply and suddenly knows: He is Davy and Doortje's uncle. He comes from Hungary. Then the girl in the picture is—

"Doortje!" she shouts.

"What's wrong?" Mr. Ami jumps off the table. "Eva, dear, what's the matter?"

"There! That same photo was in Uncle Samuel and Aunt Soesja's blue velvet photo album. Doortje was caught, and I don't know where she is now."

"We were going to stay together forever," whispers Lisa. "We've let her down."

Mr. Ami is still looking at the magazine cover. "I'll make a very pretty frame for it," he says. "I'll use real silver. Then we can hang that adorable little Doortje above your bed."

"No, don't." Freekie Two is sitting on Lisa's hand. He bows his head. "Eva doesn't want that."

"Yes, I do," Eva snaps. "Mind your own business, Freekie Two."

SWIMMING POOL

A RED-TILED SWIMMING POOL . . . EVA IS LYING next to Ali on the lawn. The sun is so hot that she must wipe the sweat from her face with a gold velvet handkerchief.

"Do you want to go swimming?" Mr. Ami asks. "I'll stay close by so that you won't drown."

"I have to keep an eye on Ali's shoes."

He bursts out laughing. "Silly Eva, those size eleven shoes have already been stolen. Come with me."

"Deep water, 3.5 meters" is written on the side of the pool. Eva walks gingerly down the steps. It takes a long time before she reaches the water. Finally . . . the last step. She touches the water one foot at a time. Then she steps all the way in and tries to float.

"Up . . . out . . . together!" she calls, but it's no use. The water won't support her. She gazes about, searching for Ali.

A man is sitting at the edge of the pool. "Hello, Eva Zilverstijn!" he shouts. "Will you come sit with us?"

She wants to wave back, but her arms are so heavy that she can't. If she looks carefully, she can see other people. Gradually she is able to recognize their faces. Over there to the left is Betty Kooperberg. Next to her is Lou Jacobs, and next to Lou is Engeltje Bachrach. Her teacher, Mr. Noach, is sitting on the side too. He claps his hands. "Come, children!" he calls. "It's time for school. You'll be safe there. Stop!" He holds a little girl back. "Only Jewish children may attend our school." More and more people sit down at the side of the pool: Uncle Dries, Omi Schillaj, Davy and Doortje, Grandpa and Grandma from Stadskanaal. . . .

"Swim, Eva!" Davy shouts.

"I can't!" she answers. "There's too little water in the pool!"

"It's your fault!" Uncle Dries calls. "You didn't cry enough when you found out I was dead. You didn't even take your little polar bear with you when you had to leave home. I gave that little bear to you when Lisa was born, and you always kept it under your pillow. Your favorite uncle was murdered in Mauthausen, your polar bear is gone, and you hardly cried at all. How can that be? If children don't cry when they're sad, there won't be enough water in the swimming pool."

"Don't be angry. I wasn't allowed to cry." She looks at the spot where her uncle was sitting just two seconds ago.

"Uncle Dries!" Eva shouts. "Where are you?"

Her body feels lighter. It seems as though she is being picked up. She is floating! She turns over onto her back and sees Uncle Dries in a yellow cloud above her.

"Good, Eva!" he shouts. "Your tears are filling the pool. Keep crying until it overflows. It's good for you. Let yourself float, but don't try to swim. That's impossible to do in water that's so salty."

"Come down right away, Uncle Dries! They're shooting!"

"It's a thunderstorm, sweetheart. Lightning is going to strike me."

"Uncle Dries . . . Uncle Dries, I—"

"Eva, stop. I can't sleep. Uncle Dries was dead even before we went into hiding."

"Uncle Dries!" Eva calls.

"Stop!" Lisa shouts.

"What are you doing?" Mr. Ami is standing on the rug in front of their bed. He holds a large red candle in one hand and shields the flame with the other.

"Are you afraid of the storm, or are you two having a quarrel?" he asks, setting the candle down on the nightstand.

"No," Lisa replies. "She's been shouting all night long and calling out 'Up, out, together.' She's been kicking me too. It's driving me crazy." She pulls on the electric light cord that is hanging above the bed.

"That won't help. Have you forgotten that our electricity gets turned off at twenty minutes past eight?" he asks. "Eva, dear, open your eyes. It's me."

Mr. Ami sits down on the edge of the bed. "Shall we chase away that bad dream?" He puts his arm around her.

"Uncle Dries?"

"No, dear, it's me." He puts his cheek against hers.

"Don't," Eva whispers, and turns away.

"Are you afraid of me? I won't hurt you. Won't you let me comfort you?"

"No."

"Then what's the matter?"

"Nothing."

"Nothing? I don't believe it. Wait. I've got to go to my linen closet. I'll be right back."

Eva closes her eyes. Lisa taps her on the arm.

"Don't sleep, Eva, please don't sleep. Pretty soon you'll be doing it again."

The door creaks. Mr. Ami tiptoes to the bed.

"Eva look at me," says a voice that she has never heard before. "Open your eyes, Eva. I've come to help chase away your bad dreams."

She looks in the direction of the voice.

"I've come to make you laugh. I used to be just an ordinary washcloth. My master himself embroidered my eyes and nose."

"No!" Eva shouts, and dives under the blanket. "Don't! Lisa, make him go away."

"Take your puppet away, Mr. Ami. Eva can't stand it," says Lisa.

"Why not?"

"I think it's because Doortje's brother made a puppet from a washcloth, just like yours. Its name was Albert. The whole family was caught soon after he'd made it."

"I'm sorry. How could I have known? I'm

now a puppeteer who scares children. Girls, I'm so sorry. How can I make it up to you? I'll . . . I'll put on puppet shows for you day and night."

"No. You shouldn't be so nice, Mr. Ami." Eva's voice is muffled by the blanket.

"I shouldn't be so nice?"

"No."

"Why not?"

Eva throws off the covers and puts her hands over her eyes. The tears that drip between her fingers are just as salty as the water in the swimming pool.

"I know why," says Lisa. "Shall I tell him, Eva?"

"Go ahead."

"Eva has told me that she doesn't want to like you."

"Why not?" Deep wrinkles appear on his forehead.

"'We're only going to have to leave again. I don't want to like anyone in the whole world except you.' *That's* what you said, isn't it, Eva? I'm the only person you want to like."

Eva is buried so deeply under the covers that they can scarcely hear her reply. "That's right," she says.

PINS

"MR. AMI, WHAT DO YOU CALL THOSE PUPPETS that are on strings? I know it begins with a girl's name, but I can't remember what it is."

Mr. Ami looks at Lisa without really seeing her.

"Eva, he's not answering," she whispers. "I've asked him three times now."

King Koerian lics with his head on the table. Mr. Ami's right hand is buried in the puppet's velvet coat, but the king isn't moving.

"Are you sick, Mr. Ami?" Eva lays her hand on the golden robe.

"No." King Koerian moves a little, then is still.

"You look so sad."

"I *am* sad, Eva."

"Why?"

"Don't ask."

"Has someone else been caught? Was there a roundup again?"

Mr. Ami doesn't answer.

Lisa picks up Freekie Two. "I know," says the puppet. "Something happened to their mama and papa."

"No, no, no, Freekie Two." Mr. Ami stands up, puts his hands behind his back, and begins to pace through the studio.

"I have to tell," he says to himself. "Until now I've kept all these terrible things to myself."

"We already know about a lot of terrible things." Lisa follows Mr. Ami around the room.

"There has been another shooting. Fourteen people were killed. Three boys from one family." He sits down and rests his head on the table, just like King Koerian. "Fourteen people," he repeats, and sighs.

"How awful."

"*Very* awful."

"Rotten Nazis!" exclaims Freekie Two. "If I had a gun, I'd kill them all!"

"Shh." Mr. Ami looks at Lisa. "What are the names of the Germans you'd like to shoot?" he asks.

"Adolf and Karl, of course. No, not Karl. Private Gröger's name was Karl, and *he* was a good German. He was shot by his own people."

"What do they look like? I mean, what kinds of clothes do they wear?"

"Members of the SS wear black uniforms, and on their collars they have the letters *SS*."

"Right." He takes his hand out of King Koerian. "I'm going to fetch something," he says. "I made it while you were in bed at night, and I can use it in my puppet shows when the war is over."

Mr. Ami returns to his studio holding one hand behind his back. "Don't be frightened," he says. Slowly he brings his hand forward. He is holding a puppet.

"Oh, no!" Lisa puts her hands over her eyes, then spreads her fingers and peeks at Mr. Ami.

"That's exactly what an SSer looks like," she says. "That evil head and the black uniform. And that's where the lightning-shaped letters of the SS must go," she adds, pointing to the collar. "Wait, I'll draw them."

She points to her paper. That's kind of what they look like. See? *⚡⚡*," she says.

"You're right," says Mr. Ami. "That's what an SSer looks like. What shall we call him?"

"He doesn't have a name." Lisa glares at the doll. "You don't have a name, you villain."

"Fine. Now kill him. You wanted to shoot the first German who came along, didn't you?" Mr. Ami sets a round tin box down on the table. A picture of a clown with red hair and a red nose is painted on the lid.

"He looks like you, master," says Freekie Two. "Why don't you ever wear your clown costume?"

"I like to wear it only when I'm performing," Mr. Ami explains. He slides the tin toward Eva. "Open it. Wait until you see what's inside."

Eva pries off the lid. "Pins?" she asks.

"Yes, pins," he answers, his eyes blazing. "Now go ahead and stick them into that German wherever you want. I'll hold him for you. Go on."

Lisa takes a pin and sticks it into the doll's left eye. "I'll save the last pin for your heart, but first I'll stick you in your other eye and in your stomach and in your tongue," she says.

"How about you?" Mr. Ami looks at Eva. "Don't you want to?"

"No," she replies with a shudder.

"Come, he can't do anything to you. Here. Take a pin."

"Stick him in his belly!" Lisa shouts. "Stick him in his belly button."

Eva takes a pin and sticks it into the puppet's middle.

"Ouch!" cries the SSer.

"Good, Eva. The doll has fallen under the table." Lisa cheers.

"Blood!" Eva calls, and kicks her chair back. "He's bleeding. Look, there's blood on the table."

Mr. Ami licks a drop of blood from his hand. "You've killed him," he says. "He's as dead as a doornail. I'm a bit injured myself. Oh, look. The pin I gave you is longer than the rest. That's why you got me."

"Take him away, Mr. Ami," says Eva. "I don't want to see him again."

"I'll put him back with my other puppets," Mr. Ami says, "but let's make an agreement. If one of you becomes very angry or sad, then take the doll and do whatever you want to it. If it breaks, I'll make a new one. Now let's put the pins back in the box."

Eva sets her foot on the SSer. "May I?" she asks.

"Go ahead. You heard what I just said."

She kicks the puppet so hard that it flies

through the doorway and into the hall. She runs after it, kicking wildly. "Here, a kick for Grandpa and Grandma and for Ali and for Doortje and for—"

"Shh, quiet down." Mr. Ami puts his hands over her eyes. "Stop," he says gently. "You've already kicked it down the stairs, and if you keep kicking the wall like that, you're going to hurt yourself."

"That was good, Eva. You remember what I said, don't you?" she hears Uncle Dries say with satisfaction. "If children don't cry when they're sad, there won't be enough water in the swimming pool."

Taking a Walk

"I wish that Mr. Ami's visitors would get lost," says Lisa, and she stretches out on the red-checked blanket. "I want to go downstairs or to the studio. I'm bored stiff."

"Then read a book," says Eva.

"I don't feel like it. Will you take a walk with me?" she asks, and begins to yawn loudly.

"No, I'm reading."

"It's nice weather."

"No, it isn't. It's raining."

"It never rains where *we* walk. The sun shines all the time."

"All right," says Eva, and she lays her book on the nightstand. "Tell me where we're going."

"To Grandpa Zadok and Grandma Esther in Groningen."

"Fine. Come on, sit up." She extends her hand and pulls Lisa upright. Then she moves next to her.

"Close your eyes," Lisa commands. "We're walking down the Folkingestraat. Let's stop at number five. 'Anno 1860' is printed in gold letters above the window of the guest room. Can you see it? We won't go inside because Grandpa and Grandma aren't home anyway."

Eva nods. Her eyes remain closed.

"Let's keep walking, Eva. Past Sjontie de Beer's pastry shop."

"How wonderful it smells," Eva whispers. "I smell vanilla and butter and cinnamon. Now we're walking past number eleven. That's Uncle Aron Stoppelman's house. There are a lot of bicycles in his shopwindow."

"We'll cross the street now," says Lisa. "I want to stop at the Hildesheim Bakery. It's number fifty-two. Come on, let's buy some egg cookies."

"So, *gebensjte kinderen,*" she says, imitating Aunt Jenny Hildesheim's voice. "My blessed children, what will it be today? Do you want some *plevekoeken?*"

"Yes, egg cookies," says Lisa in her own voice. "My grandpa and grandma will pay for them later."

"That will be on Friday, when they come to my bakery to pick up the Sabbath challahs.

"Friday . . . a white tablecloth . . . candles . . . and . . ." says Lisa in her own voice once again.

"Stop, Lisa. I've had enough. I want to read now."

"Then I'll walk by myself." Lisa opens her eyes a bit. "I'm going past number forty-nine, Uncle Louis Meijer's grocery store. I smell nutmeg, coffee, and—"

"Do you smell coffee? Yes, indeed you do."

Mr. Ami has entered the room so quietly that they didn't even hear him.

"I served the last of the real coffee to my guests. From now on I'll only be able to offer artificial coffee when company comes," he says. "And now it's time to eat, girls. My guests have left. We had a good visit."

"I didn't hear anything," says Lisa.

"Then surely you were totally absorbed in what you were doing, for we weren't speaking quietly at all," says Mr. Ami. He pulls Lisa's pigtail, then sits down next to her. "What were you doing?"

"Taking a walk."

"Oh. Where?"

"In Groningen."

"Was it fun?"

"Yes. We bought egg cookies."

"Mmm, I can smell them," he says, and takes a deep breath. "Oh, no!"

He runs to the hall. "I smell something burning! My endive. Run, children. Otherwise we'll have nothing else to eat today. Our gas will be shut off at one o'clock again."

They run down the stairs as quietly as they can. The smell is getting worse.

"Maybe the whole kitchen is burning up," Lisa pants. "Stay in the hall, Eva. We're not allowed in the kitchen! Everyone can see us there."

"Take a look." Mr. Ami is standing in the hall with a blue pan in his hand. The white interior is now pitch black.

"I'll have to throw the endive away," he says, and looks as though something terrible had happened. "Then you'll . . . uh . . . we'll eat only potatoes and meat today."

He puts the pan in the sink and turns on the water. Bits of charred endive spatter against the cabinet. "I'll clean this up later. We'll eat first. Eva, would you bring the meat to the table? And

Lisa, you bring in the potatoes. I'll carry the gravy."

"Aren't you at all curious about my company?" asks Mr. Ami when they are sitting at the dining room table. "Don't you want to know who the people were and why they came?" He spears a piece of meat onto his fork.

"Guests are boring," Lisa grumbles.

Mr. Ami lays his fork down next to his plate. The meat is still attached. It makes a brown spot on the tablecloth. "The guests weren't boring to me, and they shouldn't be boring to *you* either," he says secretively.

The girls look at each other and shrug their shoulders.

"Why not? Why shouldn't they be boring to us?" Lisa asks, and crams half a potato into her mouth.

"They were the mother and father of a girl named Marleen. She will be having a birthday soon, and her parents would like to invite her whole class to come here and see a puppet show. Our salary will be most unusual: a pound of butter. Just think of that! We'll be earning one hundred thirty guilders for a one-hour show;

that's what a pound of butter is worth now. I say 'we' because my little brunettes are going to help."

Mr. Ami stands up and bows to Eva. "Lisa, this is my new assistant puppeteer," he announces. He bows to Lisa. "Eva, this is my new assistant to the assistant."

"No!" cries Lisa, nearly choking on her potato. "I don't want to be an assistant. I want to stay upstairs. What about you, Eva?"

"I don't want to be an assistant either. I want to stay upstairs too."

"Finish your meal," he says. "Don't think about it right now. We'll talk about it later. I'll start cleaning up the mess in the kitchen."

They hear water running into a bucket, then the squeaking of a chamois cloth rubbing against the cabinet.

"It's too bad there are no curtains in the kitchen," says Lisa. "Otherwise we could be helping him."

"Mr. Ami is sick," says Eva. "Have you noticed how little he's been eating lately? And how can he let us be his assistants? I don't understand it at all."

"I don't either. And thinking about it gives me a stomachache," says Lisa. She pushes her plate away. "I don't want any more. I'll bring my plate to the hall."

"Could you please take mine?" Eva spits a piece of meat onto her plate. "I'm finished too."

Lisa walks into the hall. "Mr. Ami!" she calls. "Here are our plates." She watches as he climbs down a step stool.

"Thank you," he says, and takes the dishes. "Now run along and find something pleasant to do."

She pauses for a moment and sees Mr. Ami sit down on the bottom step and put her plate on his lap. He sets Eva's plate on the floor next to him.

Lisa can't move. She stands transfixed, as though the black-and-white floor has grabbed hold of her feet. She stares at Mr. Ami, who wolfs down the food scraps in big bites, then licks the plate clean. He does the same with the other plate; even Eva's half-chewed piece of meat disappears.

"Mr. Ami," she calls softly. "Mr. Ami."

He does not answer.

HEIL HITLER

"I THINK IT'S WONDERFUL THAT YOU'VE DECIDED to do the puppet show with me," says Mr. Ami. "And I think you're very brave too."

"It's so strange," Eva comments. "I really *want* to put on the show, and at the same time I really *don't* want to either."

He lays a tiny doll's hand on the table. "I understand your feelings, but there's one thing I want to tell you: there *are* some adults you can trust. If I say you can do it, then you can do it. In three days you'll be giving the most beautiful performance that Bilthoven has ever seen."

"Hmm," Eva mutters.

"Maybe," says Lisa.

"They're almost all inside," Mr. Ami whispers to

the girls, who are sitting behind the puppet stage. "You can see the children through the openings to the right and left of the curtains. Now don't trip over the basket of apples. If you do, they'll roll all over the floor. I'll pass out the fruit later."

"I want a mask for my face," Eva whispers.

"It's not necessary," he whispers back. "Trust me, Eva. I'll make sure that not a single child looks to see who is moving the puppets."

He pinches her cheek. "I'll be going now. Good luck, or as we artists say to one another, break a leg!"

"I have a stomachache," moans Lisa, and she presses her hands against her middle.

"Shh. Mr. Ami is starting to speak."

"Dear children," they hear, "*I* won't be the one to move the puppets today. Today the puppets will be moving all by themselves. I, Mr. Amici Enfanti, will stand in front of the stage and help you if—"

"If the English bomb our railway lines again," a child calls out. "Where would we go? Is there an air-raid shelter here?"

"Don't worry. If that should happen, I'd take you all to the bellefleur cellar," says Mr. Ami, and he smiles reassuringly.

"And what about us?" whispers Lisa.

"Of course he hasn't thought about *us*," Eva whispers back, and she slides her hand into King Koerian.

"You must promise," they hear Mr. Ami say. "No one—*no one* may look behind the stage, for then we would be taking the puppets' souls away, and that would be a terrible thing. Puppets' souls may never, ever be taken away. So . . . don't go behind the stage. Promise?"

"Yes, yes!" shout the children.

"Repeat after me: We the children, large and small."

> *We the children, large and small*
>   [say the children],
>   *Together in the Hoflaan all,*
>   *To Mr. Amici Enfanti we say,*
>   *We won't take the puppets' souls away."*

Eva and Lisa hear the buzzing of voices. All the words seem to be running together.

"It sounds like they're praying," Eva whispers.

They see Mr. Amici's back as he bows to the audience and removes his hat. Then his hands appear by the red curtains. He opens them.

"Puppets, begin," he whispers. "Break a leg! Eva, you go first."

"Hello, children," King Koerian calls in a shaky voice. "Do you know who I am?"

"No!" shout the children.

"I'm King Koerian, and I'm hungry."

"So are we!" cry the children. "Then go to the soup kitchen and have some cabbage soup!"

"Here is an apple, sire." A lady-in-waiting appears. She is wearing a long red dress and is carrying an apple between her tiny wooden hands.

"How lovely it is here, and how quiet you are," she says to the audience. "And how nice Mr. Amici Enfanti looks in his clown costume. Don't you think so, children?"

"Yes!" they shout.

"Shall I tell you a big secret?" asks the lady in a hushed voice. "Mr. Amici Enfanti has a birthday today too, just like Marleentje. He is forty-seven now. What do we do when someone has a birthday?"

"Sing!" the children call out.

"And what do we sing?"

"Long Shall He Live."

"Did I hear something? Did I hear the doorbell?" asks King Koerian.

"Yes, it's the doorbell!" a child calls. "It rang about ten times in a row."

"I'll answer the door. Carry on, puppets," says Mr. Ami.

"Shall we sing now?" asks the king.

"Yes, King Koerian!"

"It's sort of my birthday too, because I'm Marleen's sister," a little voice says.

"Then we'll sing for you too."

There are loud voices in the hall.

"More children have come," says the lady-in-waiting.

"Germans!" a child shouts. "I hear Germans and Dutchmen too. Where are you, King Koerian? Where is that fancy lady? Come back!"

"Keep going," Eva whispers. "Let your puppet say something, Lisa."

"I can't. I want to leave." The lady-in-waiting falls to the floor.

"Quick, pick it up. Keep going!" Eva pinches Lisa's arm as hard as she can.

"Ow!"

"The lady is hurt. I heard her cry out," exclaims a girl, and she climbs on her chair. "I don't see anything!" she calls.

"Remain seated, everyone!" shouts a man

with a German accent. "No one may stand!"

Two men in uniform enter the room.

"Identity card, you so-called clown," commands a man with a red mustache. *"Arbeitseinsatz!"*

"It's his birthday!" a child calls out.

"That doesn't matter. Identity card, and be quick about it."

There is the sound of footsteps approaching the stage. The boots make a tapping kind of noise as they touch the floor.

"My identity card is upstairs. I'll go get it." Mr. Ami's voice.

"Escort him upstairs, Engelbrecht. I'll stay here," says the man with the mustache.

"Boots, I hear boots," Lisa whispers. "They're coming closer. I have to throw up."

"Mr. Policeman!" cries a child. "Don't look behind the stage, Mr. Policeman! If you do, you'll take the puppets' souls away, and Mr. Amici Enfanti won't allow that."

"Sit down, I tell you!" shouts the man.

"You mustn't take the puppets' souls away!" calls another child. "Oh, look. Here comes another puppet!"

A puppet dressed in a black uniform with

lightning-shaped letters on its collar appears between the red curtains.

"Heil Hitler!" shouts the puppet.

"Heil Hitler!" shout the children.

"Deutschland über Alles!" shouts the puppet.

"Deutschland über Alles!" echo the children.

The policeman laughs; a door opens.

Mr. Ami enters the room, together with the man named Engelbrecht.

"He's coming with us," says Engelbrecht. "His identity card is not upstairs. I didn't take my eyes off him for a minute. He knows the German government has ordered him to carry his identity card at all times. This man has broken the law."

"Leave him alone, comrade," says the man with the mustache. "Everything is all right here. That clown is *Deutschfreundlich*. His puppets have just given the Hitler salute. He's a friend of the Germans. Thus he can continue with his puppet show. *Auf Wiedersehen*."

"Yes, good-bye, *auf Wiedersehen*," answers Mr. Ami.

"We'll let ourselves out," says the man with the mustache.

"Is the puppet in the black uniform coming back?" asks Marleen.

"I'll take a look. Stay where you are."

Mr. Ami disappears behind the stage and returns with the basket of shriveled apples. "Here, eat these," he says to his audience. "It's intermission now. We'll begin again in ten minutes." He goes behind the stage once more.

There is Lisa, completely hunched over. King Koerian rests on her lap; the other puppets lie scattered all around. Eva is standing next to her. With one hand she strokes Lisa's hair, which is hanging loose and looking as though she has just gone swimming. Eva's other hand is still inside the SSer.

"They're gone. Gone. I've come to thank you." Mr. Ami takes Lisa by the hand. "If you hadn't been so brave, they would have taken me away. Men my age are rounded up and sent to work in the *Arbeitseinsatz*, the labor force. They must dig holes and build defenses. Can you see me wearing wooden shoes, with a big shovel in my hand? *Me*, Mr. Amici Enfanti, the authority on children and puppeteer and so on and so forth? Oh, thank goodness, you're smiling again. Stand up, Lisa. I'm going to give you something. I'll be right back."

"There is Mr. Amici Enfanti!" calls a child. "Is

the intermission over?"

"Almost. I have to go upstairs for a minute. Take another apple."

Mr. Ami rushes up the steps, comes down again, then disappears behind the stage.

"Come, Eva," he says. "You first." He is holding two blue boxes in his hand. He opens one and takes out a gold coin. He turns it over, revealing a gold safety pin on the back. He pins it to her blouse.

"This is for your bravery," he explains. "It's an order of knighthood that I created for two of my favorite dolls. And now your turn, Lisa." He opens the other box.

"Your makeup is streaked," she says.

Mr. Ami wipes his eyes on his sleeve. "That doesn't matter. Come, here is your order of knighthood. Let me pin it to your blouse. You are the greatest heroines I know."

"Begin!" shout the children. "We want Amici! We want Amici!"

Mr. Ami steps out and faces the audience. "Act two!" he calls.

No Cabbage Soup

"In an hour we'll be allowed to go downstairs ourselves. We won't have to wait for Mr. Ami to come get us," says Lisa, shivering from the cold. "Are you as curious as I am about what he has in store for us? Maybe we'll have *oliebollen* to eat, just as we used to have on New Year's Eve."

"Or maybe bombs will be dropped on the Nazis in the city hall again," says Eva, her teeth chattering. "In any case, if bombs *did* fall, we'd have fireworks too, just as we used to have on New Year's."

Lisa puts her hand inside Freekie Two. "That's a silly joke," snaps the puppet. "Don't you know any better ones?"

"No," Eva replies, and crawls deeper under

the covers. They hear the sound of footsteps down below.

"Mr. Ami is going to the bellefleur cellar," says Lisa. "Maybe he has some food in there after all. Potatoes or carrots."

She closes her eyes and smacks her lips. "My mouth is watering," she exclaims. "Look, a bubble of spit! Maybe he won't serve cabbage soup for once. Mr. Ami told me that the pans in the soup kitchen are as big as swimming pools."

"Yes, of course." Eva brings her face above the covers, then her hands. "Almost all the people of Bilthoven get their food at the soup kitchen, and Mr. Ami keeps getting thinner because he gives some of his portions to us. And now I'm going to take a walk."

She puts her hands over Lisa's eyes. "Come with me. We already have our gloves on. Where do you want to go?"

"I want . . . I want to go to your house," says Freekie Two. "I've never been there before."

"Close your eyes," Eva whispers. "We're walking down a street. It's warm, for the sun is shining. Chestnut trees are blooming. Children are playing everywhere, and no one is wearing a star. A sailing ship passes by. The skipper tosses bread to the children. They're not hungry, so they pick up the bread and throw it into the water for the ducks. Lights are burning in our house; I can see that by looking through the windows because the curtains are open."

"Go inside," Lisa whispers. "Papa and Mama are home, and our whole family is there too. We're going to celebrate New Year's Eve together. 'A Happy and Peaceful 1945' is written in candle wax on the mirror. A candleholder with eight candles is on our table, and all the lights are on because we have electricity in the house. The stove is working too, because the Nazis haven't shut off the gas. Here is the key. I'll put it in your hand."

Eva pretends to take their old copper house key, which hangs on a circular ring with a colored photo of Papa and Mama upon it. Suddenly she drops it.

"I think it fell on the floor," says Freekie Two. Eva looks down.

"Maybe it's under the bed," says the puppet.

Eva clenches her teeth and gropes beneath the bed. "The key is lost!" she shrieks.

"Stop!" Lisa screams. "I've had enough. I don't want to play anymore, and neither does Freekie.

Let's just stay in bed. In a half hour we'll celebrate the New Year . . . downstairs, with Mr. Ami."

Lisa jumps out of bed, takes off her gloves, and lights a candle.

"Please, Eva. Stop!"

"Well . . . what do you have to say? You certainly weren't expecting *this,* were you?"

Mr. Ami is standing next to a small black stove. "It was given to me by Marleen's father," he says. "He had an extra one in his attic. We can use this stove to burn the wood that I've gathered on the sly. You haven't noticed that I've cut down trees, have you? Now take a look at what I've written on the mirror. Read it out loud."

"'A very happy and peaceful 1945,'" Eva reads.

"Come to the table," says Mr. Ami, smiling. "Who will light the candles?"

"I will," Lisa answers. "I don't need a blanket anymore, and I'll take my gloves off too."

It is so warm in the room that they are getting a bit sleepy. Lisa picks up Freekie Two.

"I smell cookies baking," the puppet whispers.

"That can't be," says Eva softly.

"What can't be?" Mr. Ami enters the room. The blue platter he is carrying is covered with a tea towel.

"It can't be that we smell cookies baking."

"You'll see, Eva. Count to three, and I'll take away the towel."

"One, two, three!"

He removes the towel. Underneath it is a small stack of pancakes.

"How did you make them?" Eva asks in surprise. "We don't have any gas, do we?"

"I made them on top of our new stove with our last . . . with the very last of our flour. But I'm convinced that it won't be long before we can buy kilos and kilos more." Mr. Ami beams and stands up so straight that it looks as though he had grown a bit fatter.

"Dear ladies," he says. "This is a first. On New Year's Eve 1944, Eva and Lisa Zilverstijn and Mr. Amici Enfanti will be eating pancakes made on our brand-new stove. Enjoy your meal."

"Enjoy your meal," answer the girls.

It is warm all around them. They listen to the ticking of the clock as they eat.

"It's five minutes to twelve," says Lisa.

"Give me your knife." Mr. Ami takes the knife from Lisa's hand. "I think that our teeth are stronger. These pancakes certainly are hard, don't you think?"

"Mmm, they're delicious. They taste just like Aunt Jenny Hildesheim's egg cookies, but they're much, much harder. Aren't they, Eva?"

"I can't understand you," Eva replies. "Your mouth is crammed full."

"I can't understand you either," Lisa says, and giggles.

The clock begins to strike the hour. Mr. Ami stands up. "It's almost 1945," he announces.

The girls stand up too. Together they count the chimes.

". . . ten . . . eleven . . . twelve . . . Happy New Year!"

They raise their glasses of artificial tea and clink them together. Lisa picks up Freekie Two.

"A very happy 1945, a year of peace," says the puppet.

SNOWDROPS

"I'VE BROUGHT YOU SOME SPRINGTIME," SAYS Mr. Ami, and he sets a small vase on the table. "How brave these little flowers are. The whole garden lies buried under the snow, yet these tiny snowdrops already dare to bloom."

He blows on his hands, which are purple from the cold. "Come, children, look at this marvel," he exclaims, and holds his hands above the stove. "Children, please, take a look."

"It's summertime now," says Eva.

Lisa is holding Freekie Two. "We're on the beach in Scheveningen," says the puppet. "It's burning hot. I'm practically suffocating.

"We're with Davy and Doortje," Lisa continues. "Eva is hiding under a big towel. She's afraid of the waves, for they're big and rough today. Doortje wants Eva to get in the water. She lifts the towel up a little, but Eva won't move."

"Do you really want to hear the sea?" asks Mr. Ami. He is still holding his hands above the stove.

"Your hands will never warm up above a stove that isn't lit," Eva tells him.

"I'll go get the sea," he says.

They hear him walking up the steps. He is moving very, very slowly.

"Did you know that the sea was upstairs?" whispers Lisa.

"No, of course not. I believe that hunger is making him a little bit crazy."

"I think I'm becoming a little bit crazy myself." Lisa draws her chair closer to her sister. "Do you feel that way too? Does your stomach sometimes shout to you that you've got to eat, or else you'll die?"

Eva nods.

"Papa and Mama are probably dead. Do you think so, Eva?"

"Sometimes, because we don't hear from them at all. I don't think about them very much. I don't even remember what they look like anymore."

"Mr. Ami says that we can't hear from them because the trains aren't running and there's no mail service."

"It's probably true." Eva slides her chair closer to the table and bends over the snowdrops.

"They smell like the outdoors," she says. "Do you hear Mr. Ami upstairs? He's looking for the sea."

"Here is the sea!" Mr. Ami lays a large white shell on the table. "Who wants to listen first?"

"I do," Lisa replies. She picks up the shell and holds it to her ear. "My goodness, I *do* hear the sea. I'd forgotten that you can hear the sea in a seashell."

"Eva, Lisa," he says solemnly, "I'm convinced that the war can't last much longer."

"That's what you said in September, when the Allies tried to take Arnhem, and now it's almost March," Eva grumbles.

"Sweetheart, I know more than you think."

"How?"

"I'll tell you a big secret. Our neighbor, Mr. van der Klyn, has a radio. Every day he listens to Radio Orange, which is broadcast from England. A little while ago he even heard Queen Wilhelmina make a speech."

Lisa picks up Freekie Two. "That can't be. You're fibbing, Mr. Ami," says the puppet. "We haven't had any electricity for a long time now. 'England has locked its door, the key lies buried near the shore, the key is—'"

"No, Freekie Two, stop singing. You're annoying me. I'm not fibbing. Mr. van der Klyn has a crystal receiver. Don't ask me how that thing works, but he says that he doesn't need electricity to operate it. In any case he keeps me informed of everything that happens. I—"

Mr. Ami closes his eyes and grabs the back of a chair. He gives a cry and falls to the floor with a thud. Then he is silent.

"It's my fault!" Lisa screams. "I shouldn't have told him that he was fibbing."

"Be quiet." Eva kneels next to Mr. Ami and taps him gently on his cheek. He groans.

"He doesn't have any blood," Lisa sobs. "Look, he's so white."

"What time is it?" he asks, opening his eyes.

"Shh," says Eva, trying to soothe him. "Shh, you're here with us."

"Walk . . . through the back garden . . . fetch Mr. van der Klyn. I'm . . . sick . . . I'm . . ." He closes his eyes again.

"You go, Lisa. I'll stay here," Eva whispers. "Do you remember the way?"

"Yes. Across the playground, along the sandbox, and I'll be at the back of number ten, where we spent our vacation."

Eva gives her a little push. "Be careful. Now go."

Lisa walks out the kitchen door. Eva returns to Mr. Ami. She tries to lift him, but he won't budge.

Eva tries not to cry, but she can't help it. Mr. Ami is going to die, and Lisa will never be coming back. She should have gone to Mr. van der Klyn's house herself. Who would ever let a small child like Lisa do something as difficult as that?

The kitchen door opens, and a man enters the room. Lisa follows him.

"I'm Mr. van der Klyn," he says to Eva, and extends his hand. "I'm pleased to meet you. At last I have the chance to see who lived in my house six years ago."

He sits down on the floor next to Mr. Ami. "Wake up!" he calls.

Mr. Ami opens his eyes. "Where am I?" he asks, and looks at the ceiling as if he had never seen it before.

"You're in your own house, where you belong," Mr. van der Klyn replies. "And we're going to put you in bed. Come, girls, let's lift him up."

They carry Mr. Ami to his bedroom and put him to bed, clothes and all.

"Can you watch him for a little while? I'll be right back," says Mr. van der Klyn, and he disappears.

"He's opening his eyes," Lisa whispers. She slips her hand under Mr. Ami's hand. "Are you cold?" she asks gently.

"Yes, a little bit, but I'll stay awake now," he answers.

"Thank goodness!" the girls exclaim together, and they heave a sigh of relief.

Mr. van der Klyn returns with a large, flat pan.

"It must be cabbage soup or sugar beets," says Lisa.

"Open your mouth, old friend," Mr. van der Klyn says.

Mr. Ami presses his lips together.

"Come on, I have enough to share with you. Don't ask me how it's possible, but the parents of my students bring me food now and then. Eat, old boy."

Small pieces of potato disappear into Mr. Ami's mouth. Each time he opens his mouth for more, the girls open their mouths too.

"He's starving," Mr. van der Klyn whispers. "If he doesn't eat, he won't make it."

"He's given all his food to us," says Lisa. "We've known that for a long time, but we couldn't do anything about it."

"Of course not." He looks at her affectionately. "Children can't do anything about that."

"And the bellefleur cellar is empty," says Eva. "What are we going to do now?"

"I'll make sure that all three of you get something to eat," he says. "Remember those parents? From now on we'll share what we have, even if it isn't much. It won't be for very long. Listen to what I say: I think it will be another two months at the most, and then we'll be free. And—"

"If Mr. Ami doesn't eat, I won't eat either," says Lisa. "What about you, Eva?"

"Neither will I," she replies. "If he gets enough to eat, he'll no longer have to lick our plates."

"So, the rest is for you," Mr. van der Klyn says. "Mr. Amici Enfanti can be by himself for a while."

They go downstairs, and Mr. van der Klyn sets the pan in the middle of the dining room table. "Eat, children," he says.

They don't even bother to get forks. With both hands they grab pieces of cold potato.

"Here are a couple of turnips," he says. "Eat a little, then stop. Don't have too much at once; otherwise you'll become very ill. In an hour you can eat some more again."

He picks up the pan and covers it with a tea towel. "I'm leaving now. Good-bye . . . uh . . ."

"I'm Marie-Louise Dutour, and that's Marie-Jeanne Dutour," says Eva, pointing to her sister. "But those weren't our names in 1939, when we stayed in your house."

"I know . . . I know, but I have an idea that in a month or two you'll be able to walk down the street and shout out your real names as loudly as you want. Now I really am going."

Mr. Van der Klyn sets the pan on the table again. "I'll leave it here," he says. "In an hour you can give a couple of bites to your foster father. Take good care of him. I'll be back to check up on you soon. Give me a key to the back door. There must be a spare key somewhere. Remember what I said about those two months.

See you later." He disappears through the kitchen door.

"He's crazy," says Eva, and she points to her forehead. "Mr. van der Klyn said that the war will end in two months. He must mean in two centuries."

ANGELO

THEY HAVE HEAD LICE AGAIN, AND SCABIES AS well. Mr. Ami clipped their hair short a long time ago. They don't care; the important thing is that Mr. Ami is no longer starving. Within five weeks he even gained three hundred grams. When he was too weak to feed himself, he allowed the girls to give him small pieces of potatoes and turnips, but that came to an end all of a sudden. One day he clenched his jaws shut. He opened his mouth only to say that he no longer wanted to eat every hour and that he could get along with less food.

Lisa put her hand into Freekie Two. "Then it will be your fault if we all die," said the puppet sternly. "We've decided that if *you* don't eat, *we* won't eat either."

Mr. Ami began to eat.

■ ■ ■

They are sitting together in the studio for the first time since the long, ice-cold winter began. Mr. Ami is perched on the table with his legs crossed, just as he used to sit.

"I'm going to ask you to do something very unusual, something important," he says. "Walk to the brown cabinet and pull out that secret drawer."

"I'll do it," says Lisa. "Eva is afraid to." She walks slowly to the cabinet, pulls the drawer out, and looks inside.

"Oh, how pretty!" she calls. "How pretty!"

"What do you see?" asks Eva.

"Gold satin, and blue and green satin, and white lace." Lisa runs her fingers over the shiny material. "What's it for? Aren't you going to save it until the war is almost over?"

"Who says it isn't?" says Mr. Ami. He jumps off the table and sits down next to Eva. He puts his arm around her, but she tries to shake it off.

"You shouldn't make such mean jokes," she tells him.

He holds her close. "But it's the truth!" he exclaims. "I'm not lying to you."

"You're silly," she replies with a shrug.

■ ■ ■

"Well, what did I tell you?"

They hear the voice of Mr. van der Klyn calling to them from their back garden. There is the sound of a key entering the lock, followed by much commotion as a kitchen chair topples over.

Mr. van der Klyn storms into the living room. "There are rumors everywhere that the Germans have capitulated and that Hitler has committed suicide!" He stands behind Mr. Ami's chair with his arms up high. "Free! We're almost free! Say something, children!"

"They're rumors," replies Eva, and she bites her lip. "Rumors are never true."

"Sometimes they are." Mr. van der Klyn tries to pull Lisa out of her chair. "Come, let's dance."

"I can't dance yet," says Lisa.

"Then I'll dance by myself." He does a strange little jig, then stops suddenly.

"I have an idea," he says. "Do you know what I'll do? I won't wait for the broadcast of Radio Orange at a quarter to eight. I'll run home and try to pick up the French broadcast of the BBC. That starts at seven."

"Then you'd better run fast, neighbor, because it begins in five minutes," says Mr. Ami.

Mr. van der Klyn rushes out of the room.

"I think he's out of his mind." Eva is sitting with her elbows on the table. Her fists push her cheeks up a bit. "Want to bet that he doesn't understand French?"

"I don't dare believe it myself," says Mr. Ami. "We'll just have to wait and see."

"Wait and see," Lisa echoes, and turns around to look at the clock. "It's almost seven. Listen."

The clock strikes the hour. They hear sounds in the kitchen. The living room door flies open. Mr. van der Klyn approaches Mr. Ami with outstretched arms.

"The time has come!" he shouts. "We're free! The German troops in northern Germany and Denmark and Holland have surrendered. Do you hear me? They have capitulated. It's over, old friend. Don't you hear me?" He grabs Mr. Ami by the shoulders. "We're free!"

"The next time Radio Orange goes on the air, will you listen, then come tell us if it's really true?" Mr. Ami asks.

"I'd have to leave my house to hear the seven forty-five broadcast," Mr. van der Klyn whispers.

"Don't ask me why, not yet. But I'll listen at a quarter to twelve, my dear friend."

"It's true . . . not true . . . true . . . not true," Lisa murmurs, counting the buttons on her blouse again and again. "Not true!" she calls. "It's not true."

"But you're missing a button," says Mr. Ami. He smiles. "It must have fallen off, and you never replaced it. Count that one too."

"True!" Lisa shouts. "Then it *is* true!"

"It won't be long before Mr. van der Klyn returns." He sighs. "You can stay up and wait for him. That goes without saying. Shall I tell you what I'm going to do with that splendid material in the meantime?"

"I don't care," Eva replies.

"Then I'll just tell your sister," he says, and moves his chair close to Lisa.

"There was once a man who could sing so high that everyone thought he was a woman," Mr. Ami begins. "He lived in Italy, and his name was Angelo d'Italia. Angelo means 'angel' in our language."

"I know an angel," Eva whispers. "His name is Emanuel."

"Mr. van der Klyn knows a great deal about Angelo because he has read about him in big books. He's told me all about this man: how he dressed, how high he could sing. And now I'd like to make a large doll for Mr. van der Klyn, to thank him for everything he has done. Long ago, when I decided to save this beautiful material, I didn't know exactly what I would do with it. Yes, I wanted to put on a huge, wonderful show to celebrate our liberation, with thirty puppets dressed in the most fantastic clothes, but now I know what to do: I'll make *one* doll for the man who saved my life. Hoflaan ten will be the residence of Angelo d'Italia, the most beautiful doll in Holland. It will be dressed in green and blue satin. It will wear boots with silver buckles upon them. Its collar will be made of white lace, and—"

The clock begins to chime.

"Another half hour has passed," Eva says, and sighs.

"There's no one in the street," says Lisa. "If the rumors are true, we can buy Scabinol right away. But if the rumors really *are* true, people would be outside now—"

"It's eleven-thirty," says Mr. Ami.

They remain silent. The minutes drag on. The clock begins to strike the hour. Mr. van der Klyn bursts into the room just before the twelfth chime fades away.

"We're free!" he shouts. "People . . . people, we're free!"

POLAR BEARS

IT HAS BEEN THREE DAYS SINCE MR. VAN DER Klyn brought them news of the surrender, but Eva and Lisa have yet to set foot outside.

"There are armed German soldiers prowling around everywhere," Mr. Ami explained. "Perhaps in a couple of days they'll learn that their generals have capitulated."

Lisa picks up Freekie Two. "Maybe Adolf Hitler isn't dead at all," says the puppet. "Maybe he's just hiding out somewhere."

"No, Freekie Two, he's as dead as a doornail," says Mr. Ami. "The coward really did commit suicide. What do I hear now? Do you hear that strange buzzing too?"

He rushes to the window. "There are people everywhere, and no one is shooting at them!" he calls. "I see a Dutch flag across the street, and I see people wearing orange sashes too! Come look out the window, children."

The girls don't move but merely look at each other. Eva shakes her head.

Mr. Ami runs out of the room and returns with King Koerian.

"It's safe, children!" the king announces. "Go outside with the man who has protected you all these months. You know that you can trust him, don't you?"

"All right," says Eva. "Let's go. Are you coming, Lisa?"

Mr. Ami pushes the front door wide open. "Follow me," he says hoarsely, and he bows to the girls. "Come on, step out. You're free now."

It is so light outside that their eyes begin to water. Mr. Ami's eyes are watering too. Tears are dripping down his cheeks.

"The Canadians are coming! The Canadians are coming! They're heading down the Soesdijkseweg!" people shout, and begin to run faster and faster.

Eva and Lisa try to run with the crowd, but they are so stiff that they can't keep up. When they reach the Soesdijkseweg, they are all out of breath. There is cheering, shouting, a tank, and another tank, with polar bears painted on the front.

"Thank you, liberators! Thank you!" calls a man.

"Old soldiers never die . . ." sing the soldiers. "They just fade away. . . ."

More tanks roll down the street. They are packed with children waving red, white, and blue Dutch flags.

"Thank you, Polar Bears!" a man cries, and throws his hat up high.

"Catch our little polar bears!" calls a soldier. Hands reach out to catch the toy bears that are thrown from the tanks. Lisa stoops to pick one up. She nearly falls over, but Mr. Ami grabs her just in time.

"I've got one!" she cheers. "Here, Eva, this is for you. Now you have a polar bear again."

The people behind them begin to move forward. "Prince Bernhard!" they scream. "He's in that jeep! Orange above all . . . long live the queen!"

Children climb up on the tanks. People laugh; they cry, sing, and dance. Mr. Ami and the girls are pushed along with the rest of the crowd. They reach the lawn in front of the city hall, where thousands of spectators are already waiting.

"Mayor van der Borch is back!" shouts a girl. "Our own mayor, not that phony NSB mayor."

"Shall we go home, or do you want to stay?" Mr. Ami asks.

"Let's go home," Eva replies.

Mr. Ami leads the way, walking with his arms outstretched to make a path through the crowd. The girls follow.

When they are back in the Hoflaan, they can hear children singing.

"In . . . spin . . . the rope swings in,
Out . . . spout . . . the rope swings out."

They stand and watch the children jumping rope. A girl approaches. "Do you want to play?" she asks. "My name is Heleen. Who are you?"

"I'm Marie-Jeanne Dutour, and I'm a refugee from Rotterdam. My parents are—"

Mr. Ami covers Lisa's mouth. "Be quiet, Lisa," he tells her.

"Dead," Lisa mutters through his hand.

"Oh, how sad!" says Heleen. "Who takes care of you? And is your name Lisa or Marie-Jeanne?"

"Both," Lisa replies. "And *he* takes care of us."
She points to Mr. Ami. "He lives at number
twelve," she adds.

"Oh. Good-bye now," says Heleen, and she
rejoins the group of children. "Maybe you'll
want to play with us tomorrow," she calls.

When they are inside again, Mr. Ami looks at
Eva and Lisa in bewilderment. "Girls, girls, I can
hardly understand it. We're free. We can sit in the
garden; we can go visit Mr. van der Klyn; we can
walk in the woods, even though the trees have all
been cut down there. We can sit in the sun."

He stops talking and looks directly at Eva.
"What's the matter? Aren't you happy?"

She doesn't answer.

"Aren't you even a *little* bit happy?"

"Yes. I guess I am."

"I'm not completely happy either," says Lisa.
She climbs onto Mr. Ami's lap and lays her head
against his shoulder. "Can we stay here with you
if Papa and Mama are dead?"

"Papa and Mama *are* dead. We haven't heard
from them in such a long time." Eva bites down
on her lip and takes a deep breath.

"Stand up, Lisa." Mr. Ami begins to pace the
floor. "Eva, you *couldn't* have heard from your

parents. The postal service stopped ages ago, and the railways have been on strike. How could you have heard from them?"

"Henny could have come."

"How? She couldn't have pulled that ambulance trick a second time."

"No, that's true."

"Tell me what you'd like to do now, children. It's your choice. What do you say?"

"I want to go upstairs to the studio," Lisa replies. "I want to paint and draw."

"And I want to take a walk," Eva whispers. "Not a real walk, though. An imaginary walk."

Mr. Ami sighs deeply. "Don't you realize that we're free?" he asks.

"Yes," answers Eva.

"Yes," says Lisa. "I saw the Polar Bears myself. The little toy bears flew through the air, and now Eva has one again."

The celebration continues outside on the street. The music grows louder and louder. There is the sound of people marching and singing.

"It's a long way to Tipperary, it's a long way to go . . ." sing the soldiers.

POSTCARD

"YOU'RE A BRAVE GIRL, EVA," SAYS MR. AMI. "Who would have thought a couple of days ago that you'd be going to the grocery store by yourself?"

"But I didn't come home with any vegetables. They didn't have anything yet."

"That's not your fault."

"No, it's the fault of that dead Adolf Hitler," says Lisa, giggling. "And I'm brave too, because I played outside with Heleen. We jumped rope together. She's coming to pick me up soon. Will you go with me, Eva?"

"She's already here," says Mr. Ami. "I hear the doorbell. I want you to be back in two hours. All right?"

"All right," Lisa answers.

"Have a good time." He holds the door open for them. "Hurry, children."

"I have an idea," says Heleen. "Let's go look at dead babies."

"Dead babies!" Eva and Lisa exclaim at the same time. "Where are they?"

"Everywhere." Heleen points to the right, left, and up above. "They're everywhere. Even in heaven. Come on. There's one in this house."

The front door has been left open. They tiptoe through a hall and pass through another door.

They see a table decked in a white cloth. On the table lies a small box. The girls peek inside and see a doll. The hands are folded, and white flowers have been placed between the fingers.

"Sweet, isn't he?" says a woman. "This little angel has gone straight to heaven. Pray for him. Here, all three of you may light a candle for Emieltje."

"Come on," says Heleen. "Let's go see the next one."

They walk a couple of blocks farther and stop in front of a large white house. The door is open. They enter and view another dead baby. It is a girl. She is clad in a white dress. A wreath of purple flowers has been placed on her head.

A man walks up to them. "Who are you?" he whispers.

"I'm Lisa Zilverstijn. That's my sister, Eva."

"She's a pretty little angel, don't you think?" he says, and blows his nose. "I'm Marieke's father. We didn't have enough food for her. Maybe she's happy now."

"Of course she is," Lisa whispers. "It's beautiful in heaven. My father and mother are there too."

"Did they die of hunger as well?"

"No, they died during the bombing of Rotterdam, and—"

"Come on, let's go," Eva says, and pulls Heleen and Lisa into the hall.

"Stop talking about Papa and Mama like that," she admonishes Lisa when they are outside again.

"What do I hear now?" Heleen puts her finger to her lips. "Be quiet for a minute."

"Today, May 17, the Polar Bears will be relieved from duty by the Royal Engineers of the Royal Edmontons," a man calls over a loud-speaker. "The change will take place on the lawn in front of the city hall. Come once again and welcome our other liberators."

"Forget about those babies. Come on, the city hall is nearby," says Heleen, and gives Eva and Lisa a push. "Run!" she shouts.

The lawn looks the same as it did ten days ago; it is so full of people that there is no grass to be seen. Trumpets and cymbals are sounding out in the distance.

"Ladies and gentlemen, boys and girls. Please give a hearty applause when the Royal Engineers arrive!" says a voice through the loud-speaker.

"I can't see anything. I want to go home," says Eva. She has lost sight of Heleen. She tries to move back, but she can't, for masses of people are standing behind her. She can't ask them to step aside, and she can't push them out of the way either.

"We promised to be home in two hours!" Lisa is almost in tears. "Mr. Ami will be worried about us."

"Thank you, liberators; thank you, Canadians!" shout the people.

"Let's try to get through again." Eva begins to turn around.

"Ow!" A man pushes her on the shoulder. "You're stepping on my toes." He stares at her. "Weren't you in hiding in the Hoflaan?"

"Yes."

"I thought so."

"Eva! Lisa!"

"That's Mr. Ami behind us," exclaims Lisa. "Here . . . here we are!" She waves.

"Eva . . . Lisa!" they hear again.

"Here!" Eva screams. "We're here, Mr. Ami!"

"There you are, thank goodness." Mr. Ami is standing behind them and holding a piece of paper in his outstretched hand.

"It's for you," he says, panting. "A postcard. Read it out loud, Eva."

"'Enschede, May 5, 1945,'" she reads. "'My darling girls . . .'"

"It's from Papa and Mama!" Lisa shrieks. "Give it here. That's Mama's handwriting!"

"Today is the best day of our lives. [Eva continues.] *Our little boat is still afloat upon this great big sea of life. We were liberated in Enschede on April 1, and you've finally been liberated too, thank God. I'm writing this postcard now, and as soon as the mail service is*

restored, I'll send it to you. We're still alive, in spite of all the bombardment we had to endure. Henny is still alive too. We haven't heard anything from anyone else, but I'm sure we will in time. Good-bye, my dear, dear girls. We'll see each other again, in health and in peace. A thousand kisses from Papa and Mama.

P.S. The mail service began today, May 11. I'm curious to know when you will receive this card. More kisses from Papa and Mama, and give our regards to Mr. Amici Enfanti, to whom we'll always be grateful. We'll come get you as soon as possible."

Mr. Ami puts an arm around each of them. "It's very sweet of your mother to have written that card," he comments. "But being forever grateful isn't good for a person. If you feel that way you will never, ever be free. Come, Eva and Lisa Zilverstijn, let's go home. Angelo is waiting for me."

EPILOGUE

On July 22, 1945, Mama wrote the following letter:

Dear Eva and Lisa,

I'm so glad that you're able to stay with Mr. Ami for a bit longer. Now Papa and I have plenty of time to find a house for the four of us. Do you know the poem I gave to you before we were separated? If I remember correctly, it contained the things I wished for after the liberation. My wish was, and still is, "That we may be united, all, / In a house, however small." We haven't found that house yet, but it shouldn't be long now. Papa has been spending so much time negotiating for one at the city hall that he is practically camping out there!

Now for some more serious matters. I find it difficult to have to say this in a letter, but I'm worried that you'll hear about it from someone else. It's about Davy and Doortje. Alas, they are no longer with us. Their parents and Omi Schillaj perished too. When you are a little older, Papa and I will tell you where they died. We learned the details from Uncle Samuel's cousin, who received the information from the Red Cross. They will be in our thoughts for the rest of our lives.

I have more news, so hold on now: Ali has survived. Henny heard that she was sent first to the concentration camp at Vught, then deported to Ravensbrück. Apparently the Red Cross wrote a letter stating that she will be able to return to Holland in a few weeks. She is now in a German hospital, building up her strength for the long journey home. What a stroke of luck that Ali is still alive!

Fortunately Grandpa and Geesje are back in Losser, but we told you that when we came to visit you in Bilthoven. It was wonderful to spend the day together at Mr. Ami's house, and it was very sweet of Henny to come along.

We'll come get you as soon as we have a

house. It goes without saying that we will invite
Mr. Ami to stay with us for a couple of weeks.
Give him our very best regards.

A million kisses from Papa and Mama.

P.S. How is Angelo?

Author's Note

The poem that Mama wrote to Eva and Lisa can be found on pages 84 and 85. It is a poem that my own mother wrote for me in 1944. Each time my little sister and I had to flee to a new address, we carried that poem with us. I have included it in this book as a tribute to my mother, who wrote the poem more than fifty years ago.